The Gift Horse

(Hardcover title: The Carousel Horse)

Sheila Hayes

For Michael

ISBN 0-590-41581-6

 Published by Scholastic Inc., 730 Broadway, New York, NY 10003, by arrangement with Elsevier/Nelson Books. APPLE PAPERBACKS is a registered trademark of Scholastic Inc.

12 11 10 9 8 7 6 5 4 3 2 1   3   8 9/8 0 1 2 3/9

Printed in the U.S.A.   01

The Gift
HORSE

·1·

Okay, maybe you would have taken the news with a little more grace than I did. Looking back on it, and being perfectly honest, I guess King Kong would have taken the news with a little more grace than I did.

But you have to remember, it was such a shock! I know my dad had been out of work for three months, and that would be rough on anybody's family. But he'd been promised his old teaching job back in September, and my mother hadn't even been looking at the want ads. She was still giving those cooking courses at the Y, things like "Banquets on a Budget" and "Shoestring Soufflés."

So there I was, absolutely bursting with the joy of life. Only two weeks more of school, a gorgeous sunny weekend ahead, and only one page of math for homework. I took the stairs two at a time (since we live on the second floor I never wait for the elevator), threw open the apartment door, and yelled, "I'm home!"

For some reason I always expect a blare of trumpets when I make that announcement. So far it hasn't come.

"Hi, Fran," my mother called through the kitchen doorway. Her long brown hair was knotted on top of her head the way it always is when she's cooking, but one piece had escaped and hung lazily over her ear. She turned and smiled at me, and I saw that she was up to her elbows in potato salad. My mother seems happiest when she's up to her elbows in some kind of food.

"A cold supper! Great!" I said. I love cold suppers. They always make me feel I'm on a picnic; it was like being out of school already.

Quickly I stuck my finger in the bowl and got a scoop of potato salad. "Yummy! Can I have some now? I'm *starved.*"

"Fran, that's disgusting. Wash your hands."

"What's disgusting?" I said, running them under the kitchen faucet. "A little ink may be your new secret ingredient."

"Thanks a lot," she said absentmindedly. "And take an apple. Your father's hungry too, so we're going to eat early."

I took an apple, but with one immaculate finger I also swiped some more potato salad before I ran out the door.

We did eat early that night, and afterward we sat around the table talking, as usual. Mom and Dad were drinking coffee, and Steve and I were telling them what we had done in school that day. I remember I had some really great things to tell, like getting an A-minus in a social-studies test, and then I had to go and spoil it all.

I went to the bathroom. When I came back the three of them had their heads together and were talking a mile a minute.

"Hey, what's going on?" I said.

My mother shot out of her chair and started clearing the table as if the house were on fire.

Now I'm used to that sort of thing. Every kid is. And I would just as soon be excluded from any conversation unsuited for my ears, since usually that kind is about unpaid bills.

But Steve was in on this one, and he's only four years older than I, so they weren't going to get away with it so lightly.

"What are you guys talking about?"

My mother looked at my father and my father looked at my mother and Steve started buttering another roll.

My father shrugged. "She's going to have to know sooner or later."

My mother sighed.

I began to feel really alarmed. Were they getting a divorce, like Arlene's parents? No, I thought, Steve wouldn't be in on that. . . .

"Well, dear," my mother began, "it's no big mystery. We just wanted to surprise you, when we were really sure of our plans."

She was leaning her hands on the back of her chair and using her cooking-class voice. ("Now, class, today we are going to learn some of the fine points of boil-ing wa-ter").

I sat down slowly.

"You're old enough to realize, Fran," she went on, "that the past three months haven't been easy, fi-nan-ci-ally."

Boy, do I! I wanted to say. I felt guilty every time I needed a new notebook.

"Well, your father's been offered a job for the summer out on Long Island at a yacht club. He's going to take it, and Steve is going with him. He's fifteen now, and he can be a locker boy."

I know how old my brother is, I wanted to say. Why were they treating me like such a baby? But then I heard myself whine, "You mean you're going to be away *all* summer?"

"Well, just about. July and August," my father said.

I must have looked very glum, because he started to laugh. "Fran, I'm not going to prison, for goodness sake! We can visit each other. You should know how glad I am to have this job, honey. I have the grand-and-glorious title of pool director, and I'm going to get the kind of tan that people in New York City only dream about!" He smiled, and then I had to smile too, because it *was* silly. Still, the apartment would be lonely with half the Davies family away.

"Can we still go to Aunt Jessie's?" I asked my mother.

"We can do better than that! We're going to sublet our apartment for two months, and you and I are going to spend the whole summer in Merriweather."

The mantle of gloom that had been hovering over me, ready to drape itself on my shoulders, suddenly lifted. Merriweather, Connecticut, is one of my favorite places. It's where my mother's sister lives, and we usually go there for a week or two in the summer to get out of the city. My cousin Brenda and I are the same age, and we have a ball. My cousin Bubsy, Brenda's brother, is only seven, and he's a real stinker, but we can usually keep him away from us.

"The whole summer with Aunt Jessie!" I could hardly believe it.

"Well, not *exactly* with Aunt Jessie," my mother said, a bit too quickly.

Here it comes, I thought. I couldn't imagine what the zinger could be, but I just knew there was one. I waited.

"You know the Fairchilds? The people who bought the beautiful old MacGregor place? Well, it seems that their cook is going back to Germany for two months to visit her family, and thanks to Aunt Jessie, who told me about it, I'm going to take her place. You and I can stay in that big, beautiful house right on the water."

The full impact of what my mother was saying took about thirty seconds to seep into my head, which was pretty crowded with news already; then I sputtered:

"You're going to be a *servant* for Andrea Fairchild? I know all about her. She's the town snob!"

"Fran, that's not a nice thing to say."

"Maybe not, but 'snob' is the perfect word to describe Andrea Fairchild."

By this time my father was on his third cup of coffee, and Steve had ducked out, muttering something about me being a brat. I made a mental note to get him for that later.

My mother sighed audibly. "Fran, you're going to find out that sometimes the perfect word is the one you're not supposed to use. And I'm sure she's not. I mean, how well do you know her?"

"I don't have to know her. Brenda does, and that's enough for me. Brenda told me *nobody* likes her. She thinks she's great just because she's got all that money. When the Fairchilds first moved to Merriweather, Linda McArdle had a sleepover and invited Andrea, but Andrea said no. Just like that: no. Same thing when Betsy Potter asked her to something. No. But she'll go to your house if you're rich, that's for sure. She only hangs out with the money kids."

"Good Lord," my father muttered, " 'the money kids.' You sound like one of the Bowery Boys."

"Well, that's what Brenda calls them, the kids that live over on the Sound. And she ought to know."

"Fran, you're just confirming what I said. You don't know this girl at all. You've just listened to your cousin's silly gossip. You have to learn to judge people for themselves. You and Andrea are the same age; you'll probably be real good friends."

I realized then that there was no chance of talking them out of it. The plans had been made, and I was expected to go along with them.

"Good friends! Ha! We'll probably never meet. Don't servants have to use the back stairs?"

I was sorry the minute I said it. I was being ugly, but the news had come as such a surprise. . . .

My father gave me a deadly look, and I knew I had gone too far. My mother just looked really hurt.

As I ran into my room I could hear my father's voice behind me. "I would never have believed it. I think we're raising a first-class snob."

We didn't talk about it the rest of that evening. It was awful. I wanted to apologize, but sometimes I find that awfully hard to do. This was one of those times. So we just sat around watching television in silence, with nobody talking. At least not to me.

But I made up with Mom at bedtime, when she came to tuck me in. Maybe I should be ashamed to admit it, since I'm eleven years old, but I still like to be tucked in at night.

I think I cried a little, which I always do when I know I've been a brat, and then she said, "It's going to be fun, Fran, you'll see." She was sitting on the edge of my bed. "They have a beautiful home. I saw it last year when I went with Jessie on a house-and-garden tour. And I'm not going to be killing myself. I'm going to sort of . . . manage things for the Fairchilds. Plan menus, cook the meals. It's a challenge for me, and I think it can be fun if we take the right attitude. But," she added, "if you're going to have that stricken look on your face all summer, it's going to be about as much fun as catching your finger in a pencil sharpener."

That always makes me laugh, and I did feel better about it then. Maybe if I thought of my mother as a chef, like Julia Child, I would see things in a different light.

I decided I was going to think positively. I'm a great believer in that sort of thing.

Some people might think that because my father had been unemployed for three months, and my mother had taken a job as a cook for the summer, and my whole family was being tossed around like confetti to the four winds, I might feel a little down in the mouth.

See how little some people know? I didn't feel down in the mouth at all.

Suicidal, maybe, but not down in the mouth.

·2·

The next two weeks went by as though everything were perfectly normal. Then school was out, and I was walking home with my best friend, Sarah McAuliffe. Normally I would have been happy, for I had a pretty respectable report card in my hand, but this year I felt rotten.

"You're awfully quiet for the last day of school," Sarah said finally, when her nonstop monologue on the joys of summer had fallen on deaf ears.

I sighed deeply. I was given to sighing deeply these days.

I hadn't told Sarah about my mother's

job. The fairy-tale version I had spun around school was that since my father and brother were going to be away all summer (true), we had decided to sublet our apartment to one of the university students going to summer school (true), and we were going to spend all July and August in Merriweather (true). Everybody knew my father was out of a job. But he was a teacher, and everybody knew about the budget cuts, so it was no disgrace.

But I figured my mother's being somebody's cook was nobody's business. Not even Sarah's.

Still, as we walked home on what was always the greatest day of the whole year (except for Christmas and my birthday), I couldn't help wishing I could share my problem with her. Maybe it would seem less horrible that way. I glanced over at Sarah, but she was staring down in concentration as the sidewalk squares disappeared under her feet. Counting cracks — it was a game we often played walking home.

If I were a real best friend I guess I would have told Sarah *everything*. But her father worked in a bank and wasn't out of work, and her mother didn't work at all. No, if I had held it in this long, I could last until

Monday morning, when we left for Connecticut.

Then it happened. Sarah said, "Give me your address so we can write to each other."

My mouth suddenly went dry. I hadn't thought of that. I didn't even know the Fairchilds' address, except that it was on the other side of town — that was for sure.

My head whirled. In a way, I wanted so much to tell Sarah. I could say, Actually, Sarah, my mother's been asked by a very wealthy and prominent family to supervise their menus for the summer. I don't know *how* they heard about my mother's courses, but she's going to be, uh, a Nutritional Guidance Counselor, and we're going to have a whole wing of the estate to ourselves. . . .

"Well?" Sarah said impatiently, with the stub of a pencil poised over a torn-off piece of looseleaf. She was leaning on her knee.

Brenda could give me my mail. It would really be so much easier that way.

"Oh, same as last year. Just make it care of Dunlap, 69 Walnut Street, Merri —"

"Wait a minute," Sarah said, exasperated. "I can't write that fast. Merri . . . weath . . . er, Conn . . . ect . . . i . . . cut," she said slowly. "I remember that part from last year.

Two whole months. Boy, they must have lots of room to let you stay that long."

That last remark really nettled me. I had the lousy feeling Sarah was seeing through my deception. But how could she?

"My mother and Aunt Jessie are awfully close," I said, "After all, they're sisters."

"Oh." Sarah started toward the corner where she lived. "Come down to say good-bye before you leave," she called.

"I will," I promised.

We had a very hectic weekend.

The student who was going to be using our apartment came over with his wife and their baby, who was very chubby and cute — much cuter than the student, who had a bushy beard and glasses.

Daddy and Steve left on Saturday. I felt miserable when I saw all the clothes they were taking, because it made me realize all over again that we were going to be separated for the whole summer.

When he had finished packing, Daddy sat down on the edge of his bed and called me over to him. He took both my hands into his and looked very seriously into my eyes for a moment before he said anything.

"Fran, your mother is a very gutsy lady to try something like this, and it means a great deal to her to have it work out," he finally said.

I swallowed hard.

"I know you're going to make us both very proud of you this summer. I know you're going to support her, and not make it one bit difficult for her by imagining some suddenly developed inferiority. Everybody works for somebody, pumpkin, and whether you're a cook, or a law professor, or an acrobat, you're still *you.* Those class differences went out with Queen Victoria." Then, as if he were talking to himself, he added, "Or they should have . . ."

I want you to know that I didn't just promise to be good. I promised to be an absolute *saint*, which made my father feel much better, I could tell. And I felt better, too.

On Sunday my mother and I packed all *our* stuff, which was a lot, since we were going to be gone so long. I took just about all the summer clothes I had, even all the things I'd hated last summer, when they fit. I also helped Mom clean the apartment, so the student's wife wouldn't tell everybody that The

Davieses had left their place looking like a pigsty.

Sunday night I went down the block to Sarah's and we walked over to Bernie's, where we get our ice cream. We walked back slowly, making our double dips last as long as possible.

But when it was time for us to go on Monday morning, I never *had* told Sarah the truth, and deep down inside me I felt very bad about that.

The familiar clickety-clack of the train wheels almost had me believing we were going up to stay at Aunt Jessie's, just as we always did.

The first ten minutes of the ride is always dark and gloomy, because you're still traveling underground from Grand Central Station. But then we came out of the tunnel into the harsh light of 125th Street, into Harlem. I know that part of the city only from a train window, but I always feel sorry for the people living there. The buildings are awfully shabby, and the people hang out of the windows just watching, as if they haven't anyplace to go or anything else to do. Seeing them, I felt ashamed about the way I'd been feeling. After all, I was still going up to Merriweather. Brenda and I could still get together for long lazy days at the beach. It would be just the same. Almost.

A half hour went by, and there were green meadows rushing past my window, with here and there a house near the train tracks that I would peer into, trying to catch a glimpse of the people who lived inside. I think maybe I'm a very nosy person.

The train pulled into the station with the weary huff and puff that those trains always seem to have, as if they couldn't make it another inch. The conductor helped us off with our luggage, and we stood for a moment, hesitating, on the station platform. I looked around, half expecting to see Uncle Phil's station wagon pull up to greet us.

"Let's get ourselves a cab," my mother said cheerfully.

But as we started lugging our bags in the direction of the hack stand, a bright-red convertible came careening into the station parking lot. The woman who was driving it wore huge sunglasses and a scarf tied around her head, so you couldn't recognize her even if you had been her best friend. But I could guess the identity of the angelic form in the back seat.

Andrea's golden hair was caught back in a neat-as-a-pin ponytail, and even from where we were standing I could see she was wearing a tennis outfit.

"Hi, there!" the woman called, with an exaggerated wave of her hand to get our attention.

"Why, it's Mrs. Fairchild," my mother said. "Isn't that nice? She's come to pick us up." It was funny how my mother and I never saw a situation in quite the same way.

I felt like a clumsy ox dragging my suitcases along the platform to the car.

"You didn't have to meet us," my mother was saying. "We could have gotten a cab."

"Don't be silly! Besides, it was right on my way. I've just picked up Andrea from her tennis lesson."

She looked at me from behind those huge sunglasses. I'm not exaggerating; they were the size of manhole covers. Not fair, I wanted to say, you can see me but I can't see you!

"This must be Fran. Fran, this is my daughter Andrea."

We nodded at each other, and Andrea moved over in the back seat so I could get in beside her with the luggage. It was some kind of foreign car, and not very big, that's for sure. We don't have a car. Nobody I know who lives in the city does, so I don't really know much about cars. And I couldn't care less.

Mom and Mrs. Fairchild talked about trains and commuting. Obviously both Mr. and Mrs. Fairchild commuted to the city every day.

It was only a short ride to the house, and I looked out at the scenery the whole way. Andrea didn't say a word, and neither did I.

As we went up the long, winding driveway, I must admit I was impressed. For one thing, it took longer for us to get up the driveway to the house than it had taken to get from the railroad station to the driveway.

The Fairchilds' home wasn't exactly a mansion, but it came close enough. It was an English-style stone house with casement windows — the kind of house, it occurred to me, that looks very grand and beautiful when the sun is shining, but would look rather spooky at night. We drove around to the rear, and Mrs. Fairchild pulled the car into a garage the size of Yankee Stadium.

As we came out into the sunlight, I could see the water of Long Island Sound glistening down at the foot of the rolling green lawn. It had always seemed strange, Long Island Sound being there in Connecticut, but there it was, and the houses that had the Sound at their back door were considered pretty fancy.

Andrea bounded over the lawn toward the tennis court on our left, a racket in her hand.

"Andrea, don't start practicing now. I thought you could show Fran around."

"Oh, Maggie, I just don't want to forget what David taught me today. I'll show her later, okay?"

She glanced over in my direction at this, as if acknowledging the fact that I was there.

Her mother shrugged. "Okay." Then to us, as the three of us walked toward the house, she said, "That girl lives and breathes tennis these days. But what are you going to do?" She made a you-know-how-children-are face at my mother, and my mother smiled.

Great, I wanted to say. I certainly didn't need Andrea to show me around.

We went through a side door and entered the biggest kitchen I'd ever seen. I could feel my mother absolutely glowing beside me. There were two different stoves and an "island" of butcher block where she could chop up mountains of carrots and onions and things, and all around us pots and pans and baskets were hanging from the ceiling. We went past the kitchen then and through a little hall, and we were "home."

To be honest, it certainly wasn't your average maid's room. It was a nice-size bedroom with it own bath, and off it a little terrace overlooked a garden.

My mother was enchanted. "It's just darling," she was saying to Mrs. Fairchild.

It was pretty, I had to admit. The walls had pink-and-white-flowered wallpaper, and the bathroom, which looked brand-new, was all pink tile. It was much nicer than our bathroom at home. But then, we live in an old building.

Andrea's mother left us to unpack, and I followed Mom out onto the terrace.

"Isn't this heavenly?" Mom seemed so pleased that I felt good just standing next to her. "I told you so," she said in a singsong voice. "I told you it would turn out just fine."

"Okay. You were right. It *is* nice," I said, smiling up at her with my saintliest smile.

But in the distance I could hear the *swack-swack* of a tennis ball being hit. It was lovely, all right. But how was I going to spend a whole summer under the same roof with Andrea Fairchild, town you-know-what?

·3·

I woke up the next morning with a terrible roaring sound in my ears. Slowly opening my eyes, I realized it was the sound of rain, a torrential rain, pounding against the French doors that led to our little terrace.

Staring at the closed doors and watching my first day in Merriweather being washed away, I felt a deep gloom settling over me. What would I do all day? Not just today, but every day for the next two weeks? The disappointment of last night's phone call came rushing back to me.

"Fran, it's Brenda," my mother had said, stretching the phone cord over the little counter where she and I were having our supper. The Fairchilds had gone out to a restaurant to give my mother time to get organized.

"Brenda? Hi! How are you?"

"Fine, cuz. How you doing? How is it living in a mansion?"

I laughed. It was so nice to hear Brenda's voice. She was so crazy, she always made me feel good.

"Okay, I guess. I have to get used to it."

"Listen, Fran, my mother says I can't stay on long and tie up the Fairchild's phone, but I just wanted to say hello and tell you I'm sorry I'm not going to see you for a couple of weeks."

Thud. A big rock landed right in my stomach.

"Huh? What do you mean?"

"Well, you know Eva Marie?"

Did I! Brenda's neighbor and best friend was not one of my favorite people.

"Well, her folks have bought a camper, and they're going up to Maine with it tomorrow, and they've invited me to go along."

"Oh, Brenda!" I wailed.

"I'm sorry, Fran. I know it's stinky, with you just getting here and everything, and if you were only going to be here for a week I would have said no absolutely, no matter how much fun it was going to be or how much I wanted to go. But since you're going to be here for the whole summer this year, even Eva Marie said she was sure you wouldn't mind. You don't, do you, Fran? Say you don't!"

Incredibly, I heard some girl sitting on my stool saying in my voice that of course I didn't mind. "Don't be silly, Brenda, we have the whole summer. Have a good time."

I think lying may turn out to be my one big talent.

So here I was, a rainy day, and two empty weeks stretching endlessly before me.

I got out of bed and pulled on a pair of shorts and my T-shirt of the week. This one had originally been Steve's, but luckily it had shrunk. It had green, yellow, and orange rings around a black shiny shark. I loved it.

Slipping into my sandals, I noticed how dirty my bare feet were, and I was sure that my mother was going to notice it, too.

"Hi," I said, coming into the kitchen.

My mother gave me a big smile. "Good morning, sleepyhead. I was beginning to think you were going to sleep clear through until September. Hungry?"

I shook my head. "Not really." I'm never

hungry in the morning, which usually drives my mother crazy. She figures I'm going to die of malnutrition if I skip breakfast. But this morning she was busy doing something to *their* garbage disposal, and it didn't seem to bother her so much.

"May I get some juice?" I asked. It was weird, you'll have to take my word for it. Was I allowed to forage in the refrigerator, or wasn't I? I wasn't a guest, yet it wasn't my own house. I was definitely a new species of person: a servant's child.

"Of course you can have some juice," my mother said over her shoulder.

Then, as if she had read my mind, as my mother does a lot of times, she dried her hands on a towel and came over and took me by the shoulders. "Fran, you're supposed to feel comfortable and at home here. You respect the Fairchilds' privacy, and you don't roam all over the house, but if you're hungry, you come in here and make yourself a sandwich just as you do at home. I have a job here, period, just as Mrs. Fairchild has a job."

My mother sighed deeply. Sometimes she gets out of breath when she starts giving one of her lectures.

There was a sound from the doorway, and

Mom and I both jumped. Andrea was standing there looking terrific in a pair of wildly striped overalls. Not overall-overalls, but shiny pressed ones with a little multicolored design embroidered into the stripes. Under it she had on a white shirt that somehow you just knew came *with* the overalls. I suddenly felt very grubby, and I folded my arms defensively over old Sharky.

"Excuse me, Mrs. Davies. I thought I heard Fran in here. My mother said I should show her around the house this morning when she got up."

My mother said, "How nice of you, Andrea. Go ahead, you two," and she shoved me out of the kitchen as though I were two years old. I hadn't even had time to have my juice.

"Okay," I said defiantly, and unfolded my arms as I followed the Little Princess out the door.

Walking behind her as she led the way into the dining room, I wondered how someone got to look like Andrea Fairchild. Not that she was gorgeous or anything. Her face was just an ordinary face. But she was so polished. It wasn't only her clothes that were shiny and pressed; *Andrea* was shiny and pressed. There wasn't one blond hair out of place, and she was as straight and tall and thin as somebody from a "Back-to-School with Lord & Taylor" ad. Even when I try to look my best (which I admit isn't often) I could never look that way. First of all, my hair isn't shiny and blond; it's just plain old medium brown. And even when I fix it perfectly, ten minutes later I look as if I'd been caught in a typhoon. Also, I'm not straight and tall and thin; I'm medium height (right in the middle of the class) and sort of chunky. I'm not fat or anything, but clothes don't fit me the way they do Andrea Fairchild. I get little bulges in them.

As we went through the dining room, I got a quick impression of a mirrored wall and a crystal chandelier, and then we were in the huge entranceway with an oriental rug on the floor and another chandelier, not so fancy this time, over my head. I could see the living room on the opposite side of the hallway.

"That's the dining room we just came through," Andrea said with a grand sweep of her arm. "And this," she continued, sweeping her arm the other way, "is the living room."

Oh, I thought, if only I could tell Sarah

about this! How we would giggle over Andrea Fairchild acting like Queen Elizabeth giving a tour of Buckingham Palace.

The living room was all yellow and white, with lots of flowers; French doors at one end opened to a flagstone terrace and the garden.

As I followed Andrea up the staircase to the second floor, I wondered suddenly what Mr. Fairchild did for a living. He must make a lot of money to live in a house like this. He wasn't a schoolteacher, I was certain of that.

The upstairs hallway was elegant with green walls, white molding, and carpeting like a lush green meadow.

"This is my mother's room," Andrea was saying, pointing to a closed door, "and this is my stepfather's. That's a bathroom, and the den's down there. . . ."

She was going so fast I couldn't get a really good look at anything, but maybe I wasn't supposed to. The den was paneled and had a fireplace, and I think the television was built into a stone wall. As I looked at it, something Andrea had just said buzzed in my ear. Stepfather? I hadn't known that. Were her parents divorced, or was her real father dead? I looked at Andrea with newfound curiosity.

She had stopped outside a room that was

absolutely gorgeous, with yellow carpeting and green and yellow flowers blooming on the walls. It was the prettiest bedroom I'd ever seen. Boy, was I going to hate my room when I got home. I used to think its red-and-white-checked curtains and denim bedspread were neat, but this bedroom looked like something in one of those magazines Mom buys sometimes.

"This is my room," Andrea said off-handedly, and then she went in and flopped on the bed. It was a canopied bed, and I don't think anybody, except maybe Scarlett O'Hara, was supposed to flop on it.

I stood awkwardly in the doorway. If this had been Sarah or Brenda, or just about any other kid in the whole world, I would have gone right into that room, because, as I may have mentioned, I'm pretty nosy and it looked as if there were a lot to see. But Andrea was the kind of person who put you off — that and, of course, the fact that my mother was her mother's cook.

Then she said, "Come on *in*," with a note of impatience in her voice. It sounded like, What are you standing in the doorway for, stupid?

So I went in, trying not to show how uncomfortable I was.

One wall of the room was almost entirely taken up with a bookshelf. On it were all kinds of stuffed animals and glass animals and, best of all, books. I had never seen so many books. Even my father's bookshelves at home didn't have as many.

I walked over and skimmed over some of the titles. She had all the Laura Ingalls Wilder books and all the works of Louisa May Alcott and then, as if to drive me over the brink, every single Nancy Drew ever written. At the moment I was on a mystery kick, and I could knock off one a day without even trying.

"Do you like to read?" Andrea's voice interrupted my thoughts.

I nodded my head.

"So do I," she said, jumping off the bed and coming over to where I was standing. "On days like today, when I can't play tennis or anything, it's the only thing that saves my sanity." She laughed, a dainty, thinking kind of laugh, the way the older girls in school laugh when some of the boys go by. "Would you like to borrow some books? Help yourself."

"Oh, no, thank you," I said quickly.

I would have loved to borrow some books,

but I wasn't going to accept any favors from Andrea Fairchild. It was the principle of the thing. I was determined to be very cool and not to get impressed with anything.

But then I turned around and saw it, and I couldn't pretend any longer. Over in a corner of the huge, high-ceilinged bedroom was a gold-and-white carousel horse.

I've always been nuts about carousels, and I think their painted horses are just the most magical things in the whole world. In the town next to Merriweather, there used to be an amusement park called Devon Rock, and every year when we came up from New York, we'd go over there one night — even when Brenda and I were pretty small — because that was when all the lights went on. The horses on the Devon Rock carousel were named for jewels, and when I was little I used to think there were real emeralds and diamonds studding the merry-go-round. They tore Devon Rock down a few years ago, and our vacations in Merriweather have never been quite the same since.

"Do you like it?" For the second time Andrea brought me back with a start.

I patted the horse almost reverently. "He's beautiful," I said softly.

"Yes, she is, isn't she?" Andrea said matter-of- factly. "It's a *girl,*" she continued. "Her name is Amber."

"I've always loved these. How'd you ever get one?"

"Richard—that's my stepfather—he gave it to me when he and Maggie were married."

"Oh." I wanted to ask When were they married? and What's it like having a mother *get* married, instead of always *being* married? and a zillion other questions, but instead I said, "Amber's a pretty name. How did you happen to name him—uh, her—that?"

"Well, *I* thought she was a golden color, but Richard said no, she was the color of amber. Actually, that was already her name when I got her. She was bought from an amusement park that used to be near her. All the horses on their carousel had the names of jewels. You know... the red horse was called Ruby, and the blue horse was named Sapphire...."

"Devon Rock!" I said, startled.

"That's right. How did you know?"

"We used to go there when I was little."

"Then you know about the horses. I'm glad Richard picked this one. It has nice eyes."

I looked at it again. Yes, it did have nice eyes. They were gentle and friendly. It was definitely not a warrior horse, like one I'd ridden on Long Island once.

As we made our way back downstairs, I felt very confused. In a way, Andrea Fairchild didn't seem all that bad. . . .

But a girl who owned her very own carousel horse! And from Devon Rock.

No, it wasn't fair. On top of everything else, it just wasn't fair.

·4·

I was just beginning to feel a little bit at home, not really, truly at home, of course, because you could practically put our whole apartment into the Fairchild's powder room, but I was getting to know my way around and nobody was bothering me. Then my mother had to go and tell me one morning that the Fairchilds were giving a dinner party that night.

It was obvious that she was very excited about cooking for those people. It was equally obvious that she never got that excited about cooking for us at home. But I tried to remember that this was a challenge for her, with the big kitchen and the fancy foods. . . . I couldn't even pronounce some of the things she was fixing.

I decided I'd better stay out of her way as much as possible, which meant I had a great choice: either read the fourth and last mystery I'd brought up with me, or do some more exploring, and I already knew every inch of the neighborhood by heart.

I would go *crazy* if I had to live in a house like that all the time. I mean, it was a lovely house (my mother kept telling me that), but it was a lonely house . . . no brothers, no sisters, no *noise*. I didn't know when Andrea ever saw her parents. They left before she got up in the morning, and sometimes they didn't come home until nine or ten o'clock at night. But it didn't seem to bother Andrea. She had a schedule every day. Mostly she was at their club, and the rest of the time she practiced her tennis.

I couldn't explain why, but I was beginning to feel a little bit sorry for her — even with the big house and the carousel horse and everything. I thought about her real father sometimes, and wondered if she missed him. I had asked Mom whether Andrea's real parents were divorced, and Mom had said, "Yes, I believe so," and that was all. You know parents will never talk to you about things like that, even if they know all the juicy details. If Mom and Dad got divorced and I had a new "daddy" — especially an old one — I think I'd die.

Mr. Fairchild was ancient . . . maybe fifty or so. I'd met him twice and he was very nice and polite. But he was not big like Dad or Uncle Phil, and he had very smooth, silvery hair and a neat little mustache. He was very dignified and serious looking, as though he thought about business all the time. I said that to my mother the first time he came into the kitchen to meet us, and my mother said he probably *did* think about business all the time, and that was how he got to have such an important job. He worked for a cosmetics company, the same one that Mrs. Fairchild worked for. I figured he must be at least the president of the company.

By three o'clock in the afternoon I was bored silly, so I wandered into the dining room and watched as my mother set the table. I have to be honest about it, it still bothered me. This was Andrea's house, and Andrea's dining-room table, so why should my mother be doing *her* mother's work?

I had almost fainted when I saw my mother's uniform hanging on our closet door. I was a real maid's uniform, in bright blue, with a little white apron.

"Are you going to *wear* that?" I had asked my mother incredulously.

"The uniform? Uh-huh," my mother said casually, as if it were the most normal thing in the world. "It's a formal dinner party, Fran," she added, as if I should know the rules, and whatever was I thinking of?

I had tried very hard to think saintly thoughts.

Now my mother was talking to herself, counting out gleaming silver knives, forks, and spoons. I'd never seen such a table. It was really elegant, with its beautiful china plates covered with pale, delicate flowers. The tablecoth was pink, and the centerpiece of flowers looked almost exactly like the plates: pink and white and green, but muted, as if you were seeing it through a veil.

I don't know what made me pick up one of the plates. As I've said, I'm a pretty nosy person, and I think I just wanted to see what was written on the back.

"Fran-cine! Put that down!" My mother hardly ever calls me Francine, and I couldn't believe she was that angry just because I'd picked up a plate. Except, of course, that it was one of *their* plates.

I put it down. My face felt flushed, and I could feel my eyes getting watery. My mother hurried down to my end of the table and wiped the plate with a cloth she was carrying. Did she think I had germs?

Then suddenly she dropped the cloth and, putting her arm around me, gave me a big hug.

"I'm sorry, love. I am so nervous, you wouldn't believe."

Right away I felt better. It's always great when your parents apologize. It doesn't happen very often, but it's always great.

"Why should you be so nervous? You're a terrific cook. They'll love the dinner," I said, really trying to calm her down.

"I hope so. It's just . . . you know . . . new to me."

I wanted to say, Brother, do I know! It's new to me, too. But I didn't. I really can stay out of trouble, sometimes.

The guests were coming at seven o'clock, so at ten minutes to seven I went to our room. It was a nice night, and I figured I'd sit on the terrace and read *The Mystery of the Hidden Mountain.* I read until the sun had faded away and it started to get dark. I finished the book and went indoors. Sounds of laughter drifted over every once in a while from the terrace outside the living room. I was dying to sneak around and see what was going on, but I didn't dare.

Pacing back and forth in a room that had suddenly gotten too small, I spied the packet of lavender stationery on my night table. Jill Axelrod had given it to me for my tenth birthday. I don't use stationery very much, so I still had four pieces left. Come to think of it, Jill Axelrod and I weren't even friends anymore.

At last I had something to do. I'd write to Sarah! I hadn't received a letter from her yet, but then there could be one waiting for me over at Aunt Jessie's, and I'd have no way of knowing. I got a pen out and started to write:

Dear Sarah,

Well, I'm finally getting around to writing to you! I know I promised to write the very first day, but what with unpacking our suitcases and putting stuff in drawers and everything, the days have just flown by. How are you?

How are Samantha and her kittens? I still

wish we could take one of them. Try not to give them all away before I get back. And remember what we agreed, no kitten to Charlie Bidwell!!! Don't let his mother fool your mother. He was only being nice to you that last day at school because he wants one. If you think your mother's weakening, tell her about that snowball fight last winter. Once she knows the real Charlie Bidwell, I'm sure she won't want one of Samantha's kittens inside their house, no matter how much his mother begs.

I paused for a moment, chewing the end of my ballpoint pen. Then I continued:

The other day I visited a beautiful house that's right on the water up here. It belongs to a girl in Brenda's class. It's very fancy, and you know what she has in her room? A real carousel horse — from a merry-go-round. I think they're RICH.

Say hello to New York for me and write soon with all the news. Miss you!!

Love,
Fran

I addressed the envelope and stamped it. Then I left it on the night table, where I would be sure not to miss it in the morning.

I wandered over to the terrace. It wasn't really dark yet, and I knew from the exploring I had done that there was a mailbox just down the road. I debated for a moment. Noboyd had said I had to stay in my room all night. I wasn't a prisoner.

Going into the bathroom, I washed my hands and face and combed my hair a little. Then I went and picked up the letter from the night table.

I had a right to my own private business.

Opening the door an inch, I could hear talking and the clinking of dishes in the dining room. My mother was in the kitchen, but I tiptoed out of the side door without being seen.

The air was crisp and cool as I hurried down the long driveway. It was getting dark very fast now. The sky was a dusky rose over the hills in the distance.

I broke into a little trot as I reached the road. It felt good to be outside. I think staying in my room was the worst part of being there. I felt as if I were being punished. My mother said I didn't have to stay in my room when they were home. But where was I supposed to go?

I reached the mailbox and dropped the letter in, feeling a little out of breath. I wasn't afraid to be out in the dark. It wasn't the first time. But the country was different. The crickets were out in force, and their eerie chant surrounded me as I hurried along the road with its giant trees looming up on either side. I liked Aunt Jessie's neighborhood better. The houses lined up side by side were near enough to the road so that you could see them at night when people put their porch lights on.

I turned back onto the driveway. At least now I could make out the lights of the house in the distance. I was reminded of my first impression: at night it *did* look spooky. I began to wonder if they were finished with dinner yet. Going around to the back door, I hurried inside and closed the screen door quietly behind me.

Then I jumped. Standing there was a large man with a bald head, a white mustache, and, unfortunately, a smelly cigar.

"Ouch!" I squealed.

"Oh, dear. I'm sorry, little lady! I didn't see you. Clumsy of me. Did my cigar burn you? Nasty habit. Have to give them up one of these days. Here, let me have a look."

There was a small red mark on my arm, but it wasn't anything to make a big fuss about. I just wanted to shrink to the size of an ant and creep past him unnoticed.

"Charles, you're heading in the wrong direction if you're coming with the rest of us,"

I heard a woman's voice call from the dining room.

And suddenly "Charles" had me by the arm and was propelling me into the dining room, where everyone was in the process of leaving the table.

"Here, look what I've done. Me and my dreadful cigars."

"Why, Fran, what's happened?" I heard Mrs. Fairchild ask.

"Now maybe you'll throw those horrible things away," a woman next to Andrea's mother was saying. I figured she was married to Charles. There was another couple, still sitting at the table, and then I saw Andrea standing in the doorway. She looked very grown up in a long, flowing blue dress, and had paused on her way out of the room with a tall dark girl who was a few years older. The two of them just stood there staring at me.

"I'm okay, honestly," I said, standing very tall and acting as dignified as I could in a T-shirt, shorts, and bare feet. "Really I am," I said, and I tried to back away from the table gracefully.

I don't know how I did it. I'd like to think that the coffee cup just hopped off the table and dumped itself on the fluffy white carpet with no help from me. At any rate, there was the coffee, oozing itself into the carpet and making a stain that grew bigger and darker every second. All I could do was stand horrified, staring at it, while somebody hurried into the kitchen. Then my mother was at my side, saying, "Oh, no!" under her breath. She turned me toward the kitchen, and I heard her saying, "I'm so sorry. . . . No, she's fine, just fine."

I am not fine! I wanted to shout. I am about to expire from shame and humiliation.

"Please go back to the room, Fran," my mother said hurriedly. "I've got to take care of this right away."

I went back to our room and switched on the light in the bathroom. I looked at my arm and ran some cold water on the small red mark. I let the water flow over my wrists and hands; then I splashed some on my face. I would never make it through this summer. I was sure of it. The way Andrea Fairchild and that other girl had looked at me! As if I were a bug. Oh, to be back home, where my mother wasn't a nervous wreck, where I was the daughter of a teacher and not the daughter of the cook.

I changed into my shorty pajamas and sat on the bed. There wasn't even anything good on TV, I soon found out, flicking the remote control. And I was hungry. I had eaten at five o'clock, so my mother could get on to more important things.

I felt terribly alone. Brenda was away. My mother didn't care about me. I started thinking about Sarah, and suddenly I missed her terribly. If only I had told her the truth. Then I could call her and tell her how horrible my life had become. At least I could write to her freely and not have to measure every word in case she should somehow discover my secret.

I was lying on the bed feeling really sorry for myself when the door opened softly and my mother came in, with short hurried steps, carrying a plate of cookies and a glass of milk.

She put them down on my night table and wordlessly gathered me up in a big bear hug. "I love you," she whispered.

"I love you," I whispered back. I peered into her face, and she looked happy. "Did the stain come out?" I asked.

She nodded.

"Did they like your food?"

She nodded again.

"I'm sorry I messed things up for you," I said.

"You didn't mess anything up. It went beautifully. Didn't you know your mother was a genius?"

We giggled, and she hurried back out to finish what she was doing.

The cookies were chocolate chip, my favorite kind. And then I found *The Creature from Planet Tyro* on Channel 8.

I felt much better. The daughter of a genius . . . It had a nice ring to it.

·5·

The days crept by, and finally one morning the phone rang, and it was Brenda, and she said, "When are you coming over?" I was so happy I could have died.

"Right away!" I said, and I was down at the bus stop in ten minutes.

The trouble is, being down at the bus stop in Merriweather is a lot different from being down at the bus stop in New York City. When the bus comes in Merriweather, it's a big event. People plan their whole days around catching the bus. In the city buses just come and go, and unless you're standing up to your knees in snow, you don't think about it that much. In Merriweather they practically have a brass band march down the street ahead of the bus.

I waited over a half hour. When two little old ladies with shopping bags joined me at my vigil, I cheered up a little. When, five minutes later, a teenage boy lined up with us, I knew the big even was imminent. And I was right. Forty-five minutes after I left the house, I was on my way.

The thought occurred to me that I could have skipped all the way to Brenda's house and gotten there sooner.

Brenda was waiting for me at the other end. I saw her as the bus pulled slowly to a stop, and I noted with a queer feeling of satisfaction that she hadn't changed a bit. Brenda's about the same size as me, with dark curly hair, and already, with the summer just begun, she had a deep-golden suntan.

"Gee, it's good to see you!" I said truthfully. "Have you been waiting *forever?*"

"No," she said, "I just got here."

They had secret schedules in Merriweather, I realized bitterly. Not fair!

Brenda's brother Bubsy was hanging upside down from a tree on their front lawn as we approached the house. As I have mentioned earlier, he is not one of my favorite people. (I am positive Bubsy is not on anybody's list of favorite people, except maybe his mother's.)

"Hi ya, Bubsy," I said, trying to be real friendly. After all, he *is* my cousin.

He made a funny face, and with the blood all gone to his head it was revolting.

We went around the back. "I see Bubsy hasn't changed," I said to Brenda.

"Yes, he has," she said resignedly. "He's gotten worse."

After I had been hugged and kissed by Aunt Jessie, Brenda and I went out back to take turns on the swing. I got to go first because I was the guest.

Brenda sat on the grass. "Is it awful living over there?" she asked, real concern in her voice.

I swung back and forth a few times before I answered.

"Not really," I said, trying to be honest. We were comfortable, the food was terrific, and Mom seemed happy, which made me me happy in a way. "It's just boring. It's not fun the way it is staying here with you guys," I added.

"I know," Brenda said sympathetically. "But I heard my mother talking to your mother. When your father and Steve come up to visit, you're all going to stay here like always. Won't that be neat?"

"Terrific!" I said. I hadn't known any definite plans had been made. Maybe Mom was going to surprise me. I missed Dad, and even Steve a little, though I'd never admit it. It would be so good to see them again!

I heard a sound behind me and turned just in time to see Eva Marie Schwartzkopf cross over from her yard into Brenda's.

"Hi, there!" she said brightly in that tinny little-girl voice I had grown to hate over the years. "How are you, Frannie?"

See what I mean? She is the only one in the whole world who calls me Frannie.

"Hi, Eva Marie," I said politely. "I'm fine. How are you?"

"Fine, thank you. I didn't know your cousin was coming to stay with you," she said to Brenda, very innocently.

I did a slow burn. I bet she knows where I'm staying, and *why*, I thought.

"She's not staying here," Brenda said testily. "I told you my aunt was working at the Fairchilds'."

"Oh, that's right, you *did*."

Now I was annoyed at Brenda. What right

did she have to blab family secrets all over the place?

I started swinging as high as I could.

It wasn't fair to be mad at Brenda, I realized. It wasn't a "family secret," and I had to stop thinking that it was.

"How are you getting along with Andrea?" Eva Marie asked, playing out the last word. "Isn't she creepy?"

My sneakers were almost touching the top of the dogwood tree. Eva Marie calling somebody creepy was funny. I could never understand how a cousin of mine could have picked Eva Maria Schwartzkopf for a best friend. But maybe when you grow up living right next door to someone, there's no choice; it just happens. I asked Brenda about it one time, and she defended Eva Marie so violently that I knew I could never mention it again. I admired Brenda for her loyalty. That was the way Sarah was about me, and vice versa.

"Oh, it's not that bad," I said. "I mean, I hardly ever see her."

"I can imagine," Brenda said. "She's always playing tennis."

"She thinks she's Billie Jean King." Eva Marie giggled.

"No, no," Brenda said quickly. "Chris Evert. She's cuter. With the *earrings.*"

I had noticed that Andrea had had her ears pierced and wore tiny gold rings in them. I thought they looked neat, but I said, "My mother would never let me get my ears pierced. "Not until I'm a teenager."

"Andrea Fairchild gets everything she wants. *Everything,*" Eva Marie said.

"Really?" I said.

"Sure. Did you see what she has in her room?"

"You mean the carousel horse?" I asked, delighted to be able to talk about it with someone.

"I mean, really!" Brenda said. "I think that's a bit much."

"Julie Farrow said it's real gaudy," Eva Marie volunteered.

"Haven't you seen it?" I asked.

"Of course not," Brenda said. "Julie's the only one from our crowd that's ever been in Andrea's room. She said the horse was painted all different colors."

"It is not!" I said defensively. "It's amber colored. It's one of the horses from Devon Rock. You remember, Brenda."

"It is? Gee, they were pretty. I didn't know that's where it came from."

I felt vaguely satisfied with myself as I jumped off the swing and held the ropes for Brenda. But I suddenly wanted to switch to another subject.

"How did you like Maine?" I asked.

"Oh, Frannie, did we ever have a ball!" squealed Eva Marie. "You should really get a camper. They're terrific, aren't they, Brenda?"

"Yeah, they sure are! I wish we had one."

"A camper's got *everything*, doesn't it, Brenda?"

Again Brenda nodded agreement.

"You have a place to sleep, and a place to cook, and a place to eat, and a little girl's room. . . ."

Eva Marie seemed to go on endlessly about the joys of camping out. Her voice rose and fell with the squeaky rhythm of a violin being played by a seven-year-old.

"And you can go anywhere in the whole wide world if you have a camper. That's what Daddy says. I think next year we're going to Australia."

"Oh, Eva Marie," Brenda interrupted mercifully, "you're not going to Australia, and you know it."

"We are so! How do you know? Maybe we'll go somewhere even *farther*."

I lay on the grass with my eyes closed, feeling the warm sun on my face and wondering if my freckles were beginning to show up again. Even with Eva Marie babbling as she was, it felt so good to be here in Brenda's backyard. So *at home.*

I hated to move when Brenda suggested, "Let's go in and get something to drink. I'm dying of thirst."

Reluctantly I got up and followed Eva Marie and Brenda into the kitchen, where we made a pitcher of lemonade.

I was glad when Aunt Jessie insisted I stay to dinner. I wasn't looking forward to waiting for that bus again, and this way Uncle Phil would drive me home.

I love my aunt and uncle. Aunt Jessie is younger and smaller than Mom and, I think, honestly, not as pretty. But she has the same kind of nice disposition, and Uncle Phil is big and gruff and tells jokes all the time. And neither of them ever yells, at least not when I'm around. I hate it when parents yell at kids in front of company.

We had meat loaf. It was different from Mom's, with some kind of peppery stuff in it, but it was awfully good. And there were scalloped potatoes and lettuce and strawberries right out of their garden. You wouldn't believe how good they were. I'm afraid I really made a pig of myself. I always get ravenous when I'm in Connecticut. My mother says it's the country air.

Before I left, Brenda and I made plans to go to the beach the next day, and Uncle Phil gave me a bus schedule so I wouldn't spend the best years of my life down at the bus stop.

Riding home in the back seat of the car with Brenda, I began to wonder if she was going to invite Eva Marie to go along with us to the beach. I thought about asking her, but then decided against it. No use knowing bad news any sooner than you have to.

But Brenda must have read my mind. Suddenly she looped her arm through mine and said, "You know, cuz, I don't feel like we really got a chance to talk today, with Eva Maria yakking away all the time. She's lots of fun, but let's just go to the beach by ourselves tomorrow, okay?"

"Sure, Brenda," I said casually.

No Eva Marie tomorrow? More than okay, Brenda. Try sensational, terrific, great, stupendous. . . .

·6·

"I still can't believe you've never been to a garage sale," Brenda said, shaking her head in disbelief.

"Well, like I told you yesterday, they don't have garage sales in the city."

We were taking the bus in to the variety store in the village. The whole garage-sale business had started the day before at the beach. We had been sitting on Brenda's towel, and I'd been letting handfuls of sand sift slowly through my fingers. It wasn't a very big beach, like Jones Beach, where we went in New York, and the waves weren't wild, as they are at the ocean. But it was a nice spot on the Sound, small and quiet, with sailboats dotting the horizon and specks of land that looked like pencil lines in the distance. The sun was making me sleepy and I wasn't paying too much attention to what Brenda was saying, when I realized she was practically shouting in my ear.

"Well, don't you?" she said, sounding exasperated.

"Don't I what?" I said, giving her a blank stare.

"Don't you think it's a great idea for a bunch of us to get together and have a garage sale? We'll make a fortune!"

"Sure, I think it's great. Anything that make a fortune is great. Tell me all the details. How does it work?"

"First of all, we've got to advertise. Signs up all over town. Then we pick someone's garage that's big and not too crowded, and we get all the junk together that we don't want anymore — like games and comic books and stuff. I've been to some of these garage sales with my mother, and you wouldn't believe the crowds. The people are lined up just begging to buy the stuff. I heard my mother say once that she'd buy anything for a quarter, and I've got tons of stuff I'm gonna sell for a quarter!"

"Gee, it sounds wonderful. When are you going to have it?"

"Next Saturday. You'll go in on it with us, won't you?"

"Of course, I'd love to!" I said honestly. "There's just one problem."

"What's that?" Brenda said, puckering her forehead.

"What could I sell? At home I have lots of junk. But I didn't bring it to the Fairchilds' with me."

"Oh . . . I didn't think of that. I guess it wouldn't be much fun for you if you couldn't sell anything."

"Well, it's still a good idea for the rest of you guys. Maybe I'll think of something."

"Wait a minute," Brenda said, an evil grin spreading across her face. "What about Andrea? Could you get some of her old stuff?"

"What? Brenda, I think you've flipped."

"Really. Maybe your mother could suggest to Andrea that it was time to clean out her closets, and then you could grab all the loot she throws out."

I shook my head. "Brenda, Andrea Fairchild doesn't have any old stuff. Her room is perfect. Like something out of *Better Homes & Gardens*. I've seen her closets. There's nothing lying on the floor but carpet."

"Gee. How can anyone live like that?"

"Well, I guess when you have that much money, you get new things constantly and you're just not sentimental about anything old. Out it goes!"

"Wow!" Brenda said, obviously impressed. "But we still have to think of something for you to sell. . . ." She stared out over the sand for a moment. "Fran, I think I've got another idea."

She did have, and this time it was a pretty good one. I was going to sell decorated seashells. I had never decorated a seashell before, but Brenda swore it was easy. I remained skeptical until she mentioned that she had seen decorated seashells being snatched up at a quarter apiece at a flea market last year. Immediately it struck me as a sound fiscal enterprise.

We scoured the beach for an hour collecting shells, then sifted through the pile getting rid of all the broken ones. I went home with twenty sandy shells to wash and decorate by Saturday.

That was why we were going to the variety store. With sequins, pearls, and a little glue, I was going to turn the common, everyday seashell into a piece of art.

The variety store was something like the

five-and-tens we have in the city — only not as big, and twice as crowded. It was so packed with merchandise we could hardly walk in the aisles.

We were headed for the notions counter, but to get there we had to pass the cosmetics bar, and naturally we stopped, just in case there was something new on the market that we hadn't heard about. There were three girls there ahead of us, crowded around little sample pots of eye shadow on the counter.

"Hi, Marcia!" Brenda said, and the tallest of the three turned and gave us a big wave.

"Hi ya, Brenda! What's doin'?"

"Nothing much. This is my cousin Fran. She's from New York."

The girls all said "Hi," and I said "Hi," and in a babble of introductions I learned that one of the other girls was named Nancy and the other Lisa, but I wasn't sure which was which.

"Try one of these," Marcia said to Brenda, waving her hand in the direction of the little eye-shadow pots.

Brenda immediately smeared something called Lilac Mist over her left eye.

"How does it look?" she asked, turning to face me.

"Truthfully? Like you just went three rounds with Muhammad Ali."

"Try that one," she said, pointing to one of the other pots. I thought for a moment it said Pea Green, and that was what it looked like to me, a miniature pot of pea soup. Then I realized it was Sea Green. I decided the one labeled Cornflower Blue was more *me*. I put some on, and if I do say so myself, I looked stunning. I turned around and showed Brenda.

"Terrific! Fran, you are definitely the type for blue eye shadow. Don't you think so, Lisa?" she said, nudging the small dark girl standing at her elbow.

"Yeah. It brings out the blue in your eyes."

Marcia chimed in, "If I were you, I'd start wearing eye shadow as soon as possible. It makes you look so . . . much . . . better," she finished lamely.

Pleased with their reaction, I turned back to the mirror, but the face I saw reflected right next to mine made me gasp.

Andrea Fairchild was standing behind me. I swear that girl moved like a cat. You never knew she was there, until . . . surprise!

"Oh, Andrea, you startled me!" I said, feeling foolish with one Cornflower-Blue finger still poised in the air.

"I'm sorry," she said. "I was surprised to see you, too."

Brenda was busy smearing Platinum over her other eye, and I don't think she even noticed that Andrea was there. The thought occurred to me that maybe she and the other girls weren't even going to acknowledge Andrea's presence.

Then Brenda said, "Hi, Andrea," very casually, into her mirror, and Andrea answered, "Hi," just as casually, without turning her head.

"Buying makeup, Fran?" Andrea asked me then, with a hint of astonishment in her voice.

"No . . . we were just fooling around," I said, wiping my finger on my shorts.

The girls stood there silently, as if they were appraising Andrea. Brenda in particular seemed to be trying to look very cool and sophisticated. The trouble was, she still had Lilac Mist on one eye and Platinum on the other, and she looked as if she had been crying for a week.

"I bet you've never tried any of this stuff, have you?" she asked Andrea, gesturing toward the counter.

"No, I haven't," Andrea answered.

"Brenda and I think it's smart to practice,"

I said cheerfully, "so we'll be ready when the time comes."

"That's a good idea," Andrea said.

"Go ahead. Why don't you try something?" I urged, in an attempt to crack the icy atmosphere that had crept over the cosmetics department.

Andrea glanced over the counter. "No, I don't think so," she said shaking her head. "My mother has drawers of stuff at home if I want it. She's in the business, you know."

"Oh, that's right," I said, feeling like a goof.

"And actually," she added, "I was just on my way over to the notions counter."

"That's where we're going," I said brightly.

"Hey, why don't you two go ahead and I'll meet you there, okay?" Brenda said, smiling a horrible false smile at Andrea.

"Come on, Fran, I'll show you where it is," Andrea said, and she led the way over to a counter covered with every kind of trim you could imagine.

"Do you have one-inch chocolate-brown grosgrain ribbon?" Andrea asked the man behind the counter politely, with the pleased air of someone who's memorized something perfectly.

"I think so . . ." the man said and, turning his back to us, he began to scan the racks of ribbon lining his shelves.

I wandered along, looking through the glass counter top at all the little packets of pearls and beads I had to choose from.

The man located the ribbon and stood expectantly before us. "How much do you want?" he asked Andrea.

"Oh . . . a yard and a half," she said. "I don't know what Maggie wants this for," she said to me, taking her package from the man and paying him, "but we're doing errands today. It's her day off." And she gave an exaggerated sigh. "Well, 'bye now." She started to turn away.

"So long," I said.

But she had stopped abruptly. "How're you getting back to the house?"

"We took the bus in," I said.

"Well, Maggie can give you a lift home. If you don't think your cousin will mind."

I glanced over at Brenda, who was squirting something on herself at the perfume counter.

"Thanks anyway," I said, "but I don't think I'd better."

"Okay. So long, then." With a wave,

Andrea made her way through the cluttered aisle toward the door.

I was trying to decide among pearls, sequins, or bugle beads when I *smelled* Brenda's return.

"My mother's in the business, you know!" she trilled, rolling her eyes dementedly.

"Oh, come on. She wasn't that bad, Brenda. And *you* stink. What did you pour on yourself?"

"Where?"

"On your *body*, where else?"

"But *where* on my body?" Brenda asked patiently. "Behind my ears I have Midnight Madness. I think that's my favorite. On my wrists, I have Garden of Desire. That's got lots of musk in it, whatever that is. And on my arms I have . . . What was it again? . . . Oh, yeah! Sidney. Isn't that a dumb name for a perfume? I wasn't even going to try it on, but I figured, what the heck!"

"You decide, miss?" the man asked.

"I'll take one packet of pearls and one packet of sequins," I said, suddenly making up my mind.

I was spending fifty cents of my allowance, but they say you have to spend money to make money.

We spent another hour browsing around the store, then hurried to catch the twelve fifteen bus. By the time we reached the bus stop, it had started to rain, and there was no place to stand to keep dry.

One thing I discovered: rainwater does not dilute perfume. Sidney, driven by Midnight Madness, was going berserk in the Garden of Desire. I tried to keep Brenda downwind of me all the way home.

·7·

I spent the next two days discovering something very important about myself. I am no Leonardo da Vinci.

After spreading newspaper all over the snack bar in the kitchen (and promising my mother for the third time that I'd clean up afterwards), I set to work decorating shells with great enthusiasm.

The first few shells were fun to do, but after that I got a little less particular with each one. By the time I had finished the twentieth shell I had so many sparkles stuck to me I looked like a walking Christmas tree.

The morning of the big day dawned gray

and ominous. I suspected that rain was not the best thing to happen during a garage sale, but I packed my shells in an old old laundry box of Mr. Fairchild and set off to find Kathy Martin's house.

The Martin house was a poor choice for our sale, if you ask me. But the thing was, nobody had asked me. Maybe Kathy's garage was big and uncrowded, but her house was situated in a part of town where there were a lot more trees than houses. *Isolated* would be the word to describe the neighborhood.

There was a sign tacked to a tree at the top of the Martins' driveway:

TREASURES FOR EVERYONE ! !
GAMES TOYS BOOKS NIK-NAKS ! !
CALLING ALL KIDS AND GROWNUPS TOO ! !
RIGHT HERE SATURDAY 10–4

It occurred to me, glancing around at the stillness of the neighborhood, that if our little friends of the forest could read — and had quarters in their pockets — we'd be a smash hit.

I stood at the top of the driveway looking into a garage where two bridge tables had been set up. One was already piled high with books and games. The other table, I guessed, was to be shared by the rest of us.

A girl about my age with long ponytails, braces, and an incredible number of freckles came bounding down the steps from the back door. She stopped when she saw me standing in the driveway.

"Hi," I said.

"Hi. Are you Brenda's counsin?" she asked.

I nodded.

"I'm Kathy. And you're . . ."

"Fran. Fran Davies."

"You're staying at the Fairchilds' this summer, aren't you?" She smiled as she said that, and I began to feel uncomfortable.

"That's right," I said.

"What are you going to sell?" she asked, looking at the box.

"Just some seashells I painted . . ."

"Can I see?"

But at that moment a car pulled up to the curb, and Aunt Jessie waved to me from the driver's seat.

Brenda tumbled out laughing, followed by Julie and Eva Marie. From the back of the car they each pulled out the assorted games, books, and stuffed animals they had brought to sell.

When the three girls saw the way Kathy had distributed the wealth on the two bridge tables, a terrible wailing started.

"That's not fair!"

"It's my garage and my tables," Kathy said defiantly.

"What's that got to do with it?"

"I'm the one whose property is being depreciated," she said grandly.

To tell you the truth, I was impressed. But Brenda looked disgusted. "Come off it, Kathy. Just because your father's a lawyer, you don't have to talk like that. And we agreed, equal space, so move your stuff over."

I thought for a moment Kathy was going to throw her body across the entrance to the garage, but she seemed to think better of the idea and, stepping aside, edged some of her goods to one side of the table.

"We'd better hurry setting things up," Brenda said. "People will be getting here soon."

"But it's only nine twenty," I said.

Julie and Eva Marie exchanged knowing looks.

"Frannie," Eva Marie said, "you just don't understand about garage sales. People come way before they're supposed to."

"Especially the dealers," Julie interjected.

"Right, and they come from all over the state, practically, and they'll *trample* each other to death to get to the tables first!"

She said this last with a big smile on her face, as though that were a sight we were all looking forward to.

I started to ask how people would know to come from all over the state when we had made only ten signs, which were all within a ten- or twelve-block area. But I didn't. I was enjoying myself, and I didn't want to go and spoil it.

When I opened my box, everyone crowded around to see the shells.

"They're not very good," I said lamely.

"Why, they're darling!" Eva Marie exclaimed. "Aren't they darling, girls?"

"I'm going to buy one; I know it," Julie said.

"You're just too talented, Frannie," Eva Marie said. "We just *hate* people like you! Don't we, girls?"

"Well, actually, you don't have to hate me, Eva Marie," I began, laughing, "because they're really not that good." And I started to point out all the places where the glue had oozed out, drowning the sparkles.

"Oh, Frannie, for goodness' sake, don't take everything I say so seriously. We don't really hate you, do we, girls? That's just my way of yakkity-yakking. Isn't it, girls?"

My ears were beginning to ring, but at that

moment Mrs. Martin brought us out a big pitcher of lemonade, and we all settled down quietly to await the thundering hordes.

By ten thirty not one of us had been trampled on.

Both Julie and Kathy had bought one of my shells, however, and Eva Marie had bought one of Julie's books. Then Brenda bought one of my shells and a pair of candlesticks with red plastic poinsettias on them from Kathy.

"These will come in handy at Christmas," she said seriously, and I nodded.

At eleven o'clock a woman came down the road with a little boy on a tricycle, and he wailed so loudly to come and see our stuff that she finally relented.

She smiled at us, and then, after looking the tables over, she said, "Gerald, these things are only for little *girls*. Come on now."

She tried to drag Gerald away, but he threw such a temper tantrum that she finally relented and Brenda scored the first legitimate sale of the day. She sold Gerald a one-legged Barbie doll for fifteen cents.

"I thought you were going to sell your stuff for a quarter?" I asked.

"I started marking a few things down a

little while ago," she said. "It starts the merchandise moving faster."

The first rumble of thunder started so softly in the distance that we almost didn't notice it. But within a few minutes it was crashing over our heads, and the rain was turning the driveway into a stream.

We took turns saying, "It can't last" for the first half hour or so. After that we didn't care anymore.

With my seventy-five-cents profit from the sale of three seashells, I bought an almost-new address book from Julie (only one entry under A, one under C, and two under H), a ball-point pen with a flower on the end from Kathy, an eraser shaped like a frog from Eva Marie, and a stuffed turtle with only one ear from Brenda. I was a little annoyed that the ear was missing, but Brenda knocked a nickel off the price, so I got a bargain.

The rest of the afternoon we sat around eating the lunches we had brought and gossiping. But I found out gossiping's not as much fun when you don't know the people.

I mean, who is Eric Caudell?

And is it good or bad that Julie's brother told Kathy's brother that he (Eric) likes her (Kathy)?

I had to keep interrupting to ask questions like, "Is he the creepy one with the frizzy hair?" which would make them all roll their eyes and moan, "No, that's Billy O'Rourke!"

As if I should *know* those things.

When Kathy's little sister came home from day camp, we all fell on the poor kid, trying to make a sale. But she was only six and didn't get an allowance yet. So we each gave her something free, so she wouldn't feel bad. We were that kind of enterprise.

It was still raining when Aunt Jessie came to take the girls home, so I got a lift too, even though the Fairchild house was really out of her way.

It was a good day, all in all, I decided. I couldn't wait to get home and tell Sarah about it. We could have our *own* garage sale, and I'd sell the rest of my seashells for fifteen cents each. The merchandise would move faster that way!

·8·

I got a letter from Sarah one day. Brenda looked at me kind of queer when she handed it to me, but she didn't say anything, and I didn't try to explain why it came to her house and not to the Fairchilds'.

According to Sarah, things were pretty boring in the city, and it was very hot, so I should have been grateful to be up in Connecticut. The trouble was, I had never realized before how busy Brenda was all summer. My vacations in Merriweather had always lasted only a week or two, and had mainly consisted of long, lazy days at the beach. But this year Brenda and Eva Marie were taking a ceramics course at summer school, and she was always being invited someplace by some friend I had never even heard of. I tried not to be jealous.

"You've got to realize, Fran," my mother said one morning, "that you're not Brenda's houseguest this year, so you can't expect to monopolize all her time."

I think she said that the morning that she pushed Andrea and me into playing a game of checkers. I hate checkers because I always lose. And when Andrea asked me if I'd rather play chess instead, and I had to admit I didn't know how, it didn't make me feel any better.

On rainy days I was reduced to reading Mom's old *Good Housekeeping* magazines and watching *Let's Make a Deal* on television. One drizzly afternoon Andrea asked me again if I wanted to borrow any of her books. Before I could think, I had said, "No, thank you" again. I wanted to shoot myself. I don't know why I always reacted to Andrea that way. I promised myself that if she offered again, I'd empty her bookshelves.

On sunny days, when Brenda didn't have other plans, I would take the bus over to the Dunlaps', and Brenda and I — and usually Eva Marie — would walk together down the sandy path to the beach. Those were the best days of the whole summer, and I really looked forward to them.

One such morning I got to the bus stop right on time, but the bus didn't. So instead of getting to Brenda's at ten o'clock as we had planned, I didn't get there until almost ten thirty.

Aunt Jessie came to the screen door, and she looked surprised when she saw me. "Oh, Fran honey, Brenda's not here. I don't think she knew you were coming."

My heart dropped like a stone inside me. "I'm sure she did, Aunt Jessie. I spoke to her on the phone last night. But I'm later than I usually am," I said, twisting my big orange towel into a knot as I spoke.

"Oh, well, maybe that's it, then. She just figured you'd follow them. She and Eva Marie left about twenty minutes ago. You know the way to the beach. . . ."

"Sure," I said, and started down the path through the bushes to the shortcut. She could have waited a little longer, I thought to myself.

The walk to the beach seemed much longer when you were alone. After I had gone two blocks past Walnut on the narrow sandy path lined with coarse grass, it seemed forever before I came over the rise and saw the beach in front of me.

When I got to the spot where we usually sat, I looked around, but I could see neither Brenda nor Eva Marie. Stripping down to my bathing suit, I kicked off my sandals and ran into the water.

I'm not a very good swimmer. In fact, even though I took swimming lessons at the Y three years in a row, I'm not what you'd call graceful in the water. I think I'm basically a splasher.

So I dunked myself a few times and looked around but they weren't in the water.

When I got back to my towel, I spotted Kathy Martin. She was with two girls I had never seen before.

"Kathy!" I called. "Have you seen Brenda or Eva Marie?"

Kathy nodded, and then, standing up, she pointed dramatically out to the middle of the Sound.

"They're out there," she called back.

I looked to where she was pointing. All I could see was water.

"Where?" I said, coming over to her.

"Out on Chrissie Bennett's boat. Her father was taking some of the kids out for the day over to Hoover Island, and he had room for two more, so Brenda and Eva Marie got to go."

I didn't know whether to cry or spit.

Kathy sat back down with her friends, and they just stayed silent for a moment, as if they were waiting for me to leave so they could resume their conversation.

"Uh . . . thanks," I said, and I wandered back to my own two feet of sand. I looked around miserably to see if there was anybody there I knew well enough to walk over to and say, Hi! Can I sit on your blanket for the day, so I don't look like I've got the plague, sitting here all by myself? But there was no one.

I put some suntan oil on my arms and legs and lay down to take a sunbath. But suddenly I felt some sand on my face and looked up to see Bubsy and one of his little friends peering down at me.

"What are you doing?" he asked.

"Uh, I'm getting a suntan, Bubsy."

"Why are you *alone?* Where's all your *friends?*" he asked, in a voice that could be heard clear down the beach.

I sat up quickly. "Who are *you?*" I asked the other little monster, trying frantically to stem the tide of conversation that was coming out of Bubsy.

But it was no use. "He's my friend Herbie," Bubsy bellowed. Then to Herbie, "She's my cousin. She hasn't got any *friends*."

"*Go away*, Bubsy!" I hissed. Then, deciding on retreat as the best move, I ran back into the water to rinse off the sand that was now sticking to my suntan oil.

Oh, how humiliating! To be called friendless by *Bubsy*.

I went back to my towel and was just settling down again when a group of kids came on the beach and stood in a bunch a few yards away from me. They stood talking for a few minutes, and then one of them — I noticed he was holding a volley ball — looked over at me questioningly. When he came over to where I was sitting, I made a great pretense of being busy wiping my sunglasses. I was sure he was going to ask me to be in their game. What else could he possibly want to ask me? I thought happily.

What he could possibly want to ask me was to move my towel over, so I wouldn't be in the way of their game. *That's* what!

I put my clothes on in three seconds flat and started back to the bus stop. The sun was hot, hot enough to make me sweat, but not hot enough to dry off my bathing suit, of course, because it was under my shorts and T-shirt.

I decided to eat the sandwich I had brought, so I'd have something to do while I shuffled along besides mutter to myself. The sandwich, unfortunately, was pickled ham, and I almost died of thirst before I made it back to the Fairchilds.'

I dragged myself over to the kitchen sink and drank two full glasses of cold water before I had the strength to speak.

"Brenda Dunlap," I said, addressing the curtains over the sink, "I'll get you for this!" Warming to my subject, I then proceeded to tell my cousin exactly what I thought of her. That's something I do sometimes. When I'm mad at somebody I can't really fight with, like my mother, or a teacher at school, I just pretend they're there. Like now, I was arguing with the kitchen curtains.

So there I was, flailing my arms and telling my absentee cousin that she was a fair-weather friend, that she sould realize how hard it was for me to get over to her house, and that she could have either waited, or refused to go on the boat, or held the boat offshore until I could dash down the beach and swim out to it the way they did in the old pirate movies.

I was just beginning to feel a bit better, when I heard a giggle behind me.

I spun around and faced Andrea Fairchild, tennis racket in hand, standing in the doorway. I could feel my face turning scarlet.

"Am I interrupting something?" she asked, giggling again.

I wanted to die.

"No . . ." I began. "I was just . . ."

"Talking to yourself," she said knowingly, and she went over to the refrigerator and got out the orange juice. "You don't have to be embarrassed. It's quite common. I do it all the time."

She poured herself a large glass of orange juice, gave me a half smile, and went out the back again.

I stood there a moment feeling foolish — also sweaty, unpopular, and slightly mad. The day was turning into an all-time super bad one.

I went into the bathroom and washed my face and, in a gesture that is rare for me, I redid my ponytails. Then, because I could hear my mother coming downstairs and I didn't feel like having to explain my whole lousy morning, I went outside.

Andrea was sitting on the terrace, sipping orange juice.

"I'm sorry if I startled you in there. It's embarrassing to find out you're not alone when you think you are."

"That's okay. I must have sounded like a raving loony."

"You're really mad at Brenda, aren't you?"

I hesitated. In one way, I wanted to blurt out how my whole day had been fouled up and how hurt I was. But to criticize Brenda to Andrea Fairchild was unthinkable.

"Oh, not really," I said. "We just got our signals crossed. You know how it can happen. Running around . . ."

"I wouldn't know about that. I'm not doing much running around this summer."

I looked at her. It was a pretty queer thing for her to say.

"Debbie and I always have a million things going on, but her parents took her to Spain for the summer. Isn't that the most grotesque thing? Spain? For the whole summer?"

"Who's Debbie?" I asked.

"Oh, I'm sorry. Of course you couldn't know her. Debbie Spencer. She's my best friend. She's terrific. We became friends right away, because luckily she moved here just about the same time I did. There aren't many kids around here, and it's a little hard . . ."

She broke off then, letting her voice trail away in the afternoon stillness.

"There's lots of nice kids in Merriweather," I said. "You should have made a lot of friends by now." After I said that I realized it wasn't too tactful a thing to bring up.

"Well, Maggie and Richard can make it pretty difficult sometimes. I mean, they're not around very much, and they like me to stay pretty close to home. So it's no to camping trips, no to slumber parties, no to anything where they don't know everybody personally. And they're never around to meet anybody! That's why I was so glad to meet Debbie. Her parents belong to the same club, so she passed muster."

She laughed then, but it wasn't a happy laugh, if you know what I mean. All those noes . . . they were her parents' fault, not hers. I'd have to tell Brenda that.

"You don't know how great it is having your mother here," she said. "She's super."

I felt really good when she said that, and I smiled.

"Thank you," I said.

"It's the truth. Bertha — that's our regular cook — she's a tyrant. She has this thick German accent, and every time I leave the house she thinks I'll get mugged. Around here

— can you believe it? *Mugged!* 'Or verse!' That's what she likes to shout at me as I go out the door. . . . 'Or verse!' "

We were both laughing when suddenly she jumped up and went over to the backboard and started practicing her tennis again.

"You like tennis a lot, don't you?" I said.

Swack . . . swack. She didn't seem to take her eye off the ball for a minute, yet she kept up her part of the conversation.

"I ab-so-lute-ly adore it. David — that's my teacher — he says I'm a natural. That's very important, you know."

She missed a shot and stopped, out of breath, brushing a few strands of blond hair off her face.

I know that part about being a natural sounds conceited, but that's what she said. At the time, I didn't think it was bad of her to say that. It just sounded true.

"What do *you* like to do?" she asked, looking at me very intently.

I had the uncomfortable feeling she honestly expected me to answer, I fly my own plane.

Andrea Fairchild looked delicate, but I was beginning to realize she had something very tough about her. Maybe *tough* isn't the right word. No, *strong* is better.

I still hadn't answered her question, and she continued to look at me, her head cocked to one side, as if I were something very interesting she had just discovered on a nature hike.

"I . . . uh . . . read . . ." I said. (Yes, I know you could die at such a dumb answer. But wait, it gets worse.) "And I ride my bike a lot." And then I got cute. "Oh, and I ride horses, too." Twice. In Central Park.

"Do you like to ride? Maybe we could go out someday. We could take a couple of horses from Scrubby Neck Farm and ride along the Point. It's a terrific ride."

As I said, I have been on a horse twice. And once the horse was a pony. Egad, I thought, is there nothing Andrea Fairchild doesn't do? No wonder nobody likes her!

"Uh, well, maybe," I said vaguely, as though the idea of galloping along the Point were a bit boring. I excused myself before I could get into any more trouble.

That night I lay in bed listening to the crickets. I know that people in the country are hardly aware of them, and that the noise I take for granted, like traffic, drives some people crazy. Still, crickets are so *noisy.*

I was half asleep and I was thinking about

how accomplished Andrea was and what a klutz *I* was. And then I had this wonderful fantasy, where Andrea and I go to school together and I get all A's (which I do, most of the time), and she can barely get C's. She even gets some D's. The teacher asks me to tutor her, because she's going to fail for sure. I really began to enjoy this sort of daydream, because — who could tell? — maybe she *wasn't* so great in school.

By the time I drifted off to sleep I had convinced myself that Wonder Woman was a complete idiot, and I felt much better about everything.

9

Brenda called the next morning. I figured I'd let her squirm a little and apologize a lot before I finally forgave her.

Why don't conversations ever go the way they're planned?

"Hello," I said, in what I hoped was a very cold calculating tone of voice.

"Hi! Whatcha doing?"

"Eating breakfast."

"I just finished. What're you having?"

"Scrambled eggs."

"Me, too! Boy, did I eat like a pig."

"They say the sea air gives one an appetite."

"Uh . . . yeah. All I had yesterday was one dinky little sandwich. All day! And we didn't get home until seven thirty."

"Oh, that's a shame."

"Fran, are you *mad?*"

"*Me?* Of course not. Why should I be mad?"

"I *knew* you'd be mad. When my mother told me you'd been here, I knew you were going to be mad. That's why I didn't call you last night. I figured you'd be over it by this morning."

I let silence hang in the air like a brick wall between us.

"Fran, I'm sorry. Honest. When you were late, we figured you weren't coming. And then, when Chrissie's father offered. . . Well, he had to go right then or miss the chance."

I am not, by nature, a hardhearted person. And Brenda *is* a blood relative. So it was not surprising that I felt a burst of compassion beginning to well up inside me.

Then she had to go and say, "Actually, Fran, if anybody has a right to be mad, it's me and Eva Marie."

"What?"

"Well, just think about it a minute. If we had waited for you five minutes more — just five minutes — we would have missed going on the boat completely!"

"Brenda Dunlap, if you think *I'm* going to apologize when you know how hard it is for me to get over there . . ."

"Oh, come on, Fran! It's not my fault you're stuck over at the Fairchilds'!"

Well, that did it, of course. *Nobody* was going to make smart remarks about my mother's being the Fairchilds' cook.

I slammed the phone down so hard that for a second I was afraid I might have broken it. I could feel my eyes filling up with tears, and I felt just miserable. Why hadn't she given me a chance to forgive her as I was going to do? The only friend I had in this whole lousy town — in the whole crummy *state* — and now we were finished forever.

I went back into the kitchen, and I guess I wasn't too successful at putting on a false front.

"What happened?" my mother asked. "You and Brenda have a fight?"

I shrugged my shoulders.

My mother turned off the water and leaned her hands on the edge of the sink. She didn't look at me, but seemed to be studying the copper pots on the windowsill.

"I know this isn't the easiest setup in the world, Fran, but quite frankly, dear, you could be a great deal worse off!"

Surprised, I looked at my mother. She sounded a little bit annoyed.

"All I want to say is . . . I had hoped you'd be better adjusted by now. I think you're making things unnecessarily hard on yourself with that chip on your shoulder."

"Me? A chip on my shoulder?" I said incredulously.

She looked at me and smiled. "Maybe I'm wrong. Anyway, want some good news?"

Boy, did I! "Like what?" I asked.

"Like Daddy and Steve coming up next weekend."

"Oh, wow! Really? Honest?"

I ran over and gave my mother a big hug. Suddenly the world was beautiful again. It would be so good to see them. Even Steve.

"Mrs. Davies?" Andrea's voice came softly from the doorway. "I wonder if I could bother you for a moment? I can't fasten this."

There could be absolutely no doubt in anyone's mind about where Andrea was going. She was wearing a long-sleeved blouse with a detachable collar (that was what needed fastening), riding breeches, and boots.

She looked like something out of *National Velvet.*

As my mother fastened the collar, she asked casually, "Going riding again, Andrea?"

"Uh-huh. It's a great day for it. Not too hot." Then Andrea suddenly looked at me. "Are you going to the beach with Brenda today?"

"Oh, I don't know," I said vaguely.

"Are you, Fran? I thought you weren't going to see Brenda today, dear." My mother was using her don't-tell-a-lie-or-you-won't-go-to-heaven tone of voice.

"Well, probably I won't be seeing *Brenda,*" I said.

"Then why don't you come with me?" Andrea said eagerly. "I promise you'll love it. You can ride Thunder. That's Debbie's horse."

"Thunder?" I repeated. My voice sounded like someone with a mouthful of marbles talking from the bottom of a well.

A note of caution suddenly crept into my mother's voice. "Oh, Andrea, that's very nice of you, but maybe it's not such a good idea. Fran is only a beginner. . . ."

Andrea laughed. "Oh, don't worry, Mrs. Davies. Thunder is a real pussycat!"

"Are you sure, Andrea?"

"Honestly, Mrs. Davies. And we'll take Charlie with us. That's the girl who takes care of the horses at Scrubby Neck."

"Well, I guess then it would be all right," my mother said, looking reassured, which was easy for her, since she didn't have to go.

I thought of saying gaily, "Mom, why don't I stay here and cook, and you go ride Thunder?"

But I didn't. What I said was, "I'll be ready in a minute."

"I don't have riding pants," I said, as we started down the road. "Sorry. Jeans are the best I can do."

"Oh, don't be silly. I'd rather wear jeans, but Richard bought these for me, so Maggie says I should wear them."

We were silent for a few moments, and I began wondering how far it was to this Scrubby Neck Farm.

"Is it a long walk?" I asked finally.

"No . . . about a mile."

"Oh," I said.

More silence.

"Your father's coming up next weekend, isn't he?" she asked. Then, as if she felt she had to apologize for knowing my personal business, she added, "I couldn't help overhearing your mother. But I knew it already. I heard Maggie telling Richard that your mother won't be at the house then, because your father's coming up and you're going to be at your aunt's. I bet you're looking forward to seeing him."

"I sure am," I said truthfully. "It's been over a month."

"You get used to it after a while. I used to miss my father a real lot. But you get used to it."

When we got to the stables, Andrea greeted a short, stocky girl who wore her thick black hair in a giant pigtail down her back.

"Hi, Charlie," she said.

"Hi." The girl smiled at Andrea. "You want Gwendolyn?"

"Yes, and could you saddle Thunder for my friend?"

The girl went off down a sawdust path between the horses' stalls.

When Charlie led Gwendolyn out, I could see that Andrea was crazy about the small light-colored horse. I thought she was pretty ordinary looking myself, but I said, "She's lovely."

Andrea nodded in quick agreement. She

was patting the horse, and the horse was nuzzling her. They seemed to be passing the time of day together.

When Charlie reappeared, leading the large, jet-black Thunder, I knew immediately that mine was the more handsome animal. I also knew immediately that I should never have hung up on Brenda.

"Here he is," Charlie said, good-naturedly. "You *have* ridden before, haven't you?" She looked at me suspiciously, as if some sixth sense told her that what I had ridden before was the crosstown bus.

"Sure," I said quickly. Then I added, "A little."

Andrea hopped on Gwendolyn as though she were riding a bicycle, while Charlie stood patiently, holding the reins of my horse and waiting for me to mount. I just stared up at the saddle for a moment.

"Need a hand getting on?" Charlie asked.

"No," I said, "but I was wondering. . . . Do you have a ladder?" Then I laughed shakily, so she'd know I was only *joking.*

I did get on, finally, and that funny feeling, as if I were sitting on top of the Empire State Building, came right back to me.

As soon as I had mounted, Thunder started snorting and stomping his feet.

Charlie pulled sharply on the reins. "Now you cut that out!" she said to the horse. Then to me she said, "Don't take any funny business from him. He's gentle as a lamb, but he likes to show off for strangers."

I thought I was going to faint.

Andrea was moving her horse around easily, and as she turned to face me — I was frozen to the spot — I said, "I thought Thunder was a pussycat?"

"Oh, he is!" she said. "You know why he's acting cranky? I bet he misses Debbie. Charlie, Fran hasn't done that much riding lately, so could you come with us this morning?"

"Sure. Just let me tell the boss and throw a saddle on Old Barney.

Old Barney. Now *that* sounded like my kind of horse.

As I've mentioned, I was frozen, and I stayed that way even after the three of us started single file down the little path through the woods to the beach. I was just beginning to thaw out a bit, just beginning to release the death grip I had on the saddle, just beginning to look around and appreciate the warm sunshine, the blue sky, the gentle breeze, when we started riding along the beach.

Charlie's horse rode quietly along the water's edge; Andrea's horse followed obediently. But Thunder? As soon as we got near the water, it was Thunder's turn to freeze. He just refused to budge. I thought for a moment he had taken root in the sand. I tried doing that clever little thing with my heels, but he ignored me. I pleaded with him, but obviously I don't talk Horse very well, because it got me nowhere. The others were going farther and farther along the beach. I called out to them, but my voice came out high and thin, and the wind whipped it away before it reached them. I glanced nervously out at the Sound. At any moment I expected Old Pussycat to make a right turn and go charging toward England.

Then I saw Charlie look around to check on my progress. What she saw, of course, was that I wasn't making any. She turned back with Andrea and came up to me, shaking her head.

"Isn't he something?" she said. "He never did like to get his feet wet!"

She got him moving again, but for the rest of the ride I kept wondering what would have happened if the tide had come in.

But since I couldn't be writing this from the grave, it goes without saying that I survived. Still, I don't think Thunder and I were really meant for each other. Of course, I'm no judge of horseflesh, and compared to the Central Park pony, anything would have seemed wild and untamed, I guess. But I do think Thunder and I had a personality conflict.

The walk home afterward was very long, and I know now why cowboys walk the way they do.

"I'm sorry," I said to Andrea. "I guess it wasn't much fun for you. I mean, I wasn't able to go very fast or anything."

Andrea was very sympathetic. "Don't be silly. I'm so glad you came with me. It doesn't matter how fast we went. Maybe I shouldn't have given you Thunder."

"No . . ." I said, "I shouldn't have pretended I was a good rider."

"But you are! I mean for someone from the city . . ."

And we both laughed.

Andrea's parents weren't going to be home that night, so my mother invited her to eat with us.

It was funny the way Andrea seemed to enjoy being with my mother. I mean, Mom didn't treat her special or anything. In fact, the more my mother nagged her to finish all her broccoli, and not to put so much salt on her meat, the more Andrea just sat there and beamed.

The two of them had a great time teasing me. Of course, I guess I made it easy for them since I had to *stand* for the whole meal.

"You know what would be good, Fran," my mother said. "Run a nice hot bath and just sit and soak for a while with a good book. You'll feel fine."

"I think I'll do that," I said wearily, limping out of the kitchen. Then I surprised myself. Turning around, I said, "Andrea, speaking of good books . . ."

·10·

I learned so much that week, became so wise in the ways of the world, that to tell you the truth I could hardly stand myself.

It was only days after we went riding that I found myself sitting up in bed one night, determined to remember everything that had happened to me that day at the Merriweather Country Club. I wanted to write it down, memorize it, and never, ever forget it!

THINGS I LEARNED AT THE MCC
OR THE ADVANTAGES OF BEING RICH
LIKE ANDREA FAIRCHILDS

1 *If you're rich* . . . you pay so much money for private lessons (in things like

tennis, for instance) that the teacher has to act real nice for the whole hour and can't moan or yell at you no matter how many times you miss the ball.

2 *If you're rich* . . . everybody — even waiters — calls you Miss Fairchild and treats you just as if you were your mother, or some other elder person.

3 *If you're rich* . . . you get to dress in your own private room, called a "cabana" — and not in a big sweaty locker room full of puddles like the ones they have at some New York City beaches I could mention.

4 *If you're rich* . . . you're independent. I used to think *I* was pretty independent, going to the store, or to Bernie's for ice cream, or to the library by myself. But those things loom absolutely sooty next to the things Andrea Fairchild does. Would you believe she signed for the lunch?

To think that when I woke up that morning — to sunshine after two days of rain — my greatest ambition had been to go to the beach with Brenda Dunlap. In fact, I came *that* close to calling her and making up. Brenda had suffered enough, I reasoned; it wasn't fair to torture her anymore. I told myself that to err was human, but to call Brenda and forgive her would be divine.

I was sitting by the telephone, staring at it

and *willing* it to ring, when Andrea bounced into the kitchen.

"Boy, doesn't that sun look good!" she said cheerfully.

"Yeah," I said halfheartedly, "but it's going to be awfully hot. The weatherman said it's going to go into the nineties."

"Yikes! I'm glad I've got a lesson scheduled for this morning before it gets too bad."

She got herself some juice and looked at me a moment.

"Going to the beach?"

"Uh . . . I don't know," I answered truthfully.

My mother was pretending to be busy at the sink, but her ears were beginning to swell like radar antennas.

"You'll probably go. It's such a gorgeous day. Unless" . . . she lowered her voice conspiratorially . . . "you and Brenda are still mad at each other?"

"Of course not!" I snapped.

We were on opposite sides again, I thought. Here was Andrea going off to play tennis (followed no doubt by a cooling dip in the Club pool), and while I was stuck in this air-conditioned tomb for the third day in a row.

"It might be boring for you just watching me take a lesson," Andrea said, "but if you have nothing else to do, do you want to come to the Club with me? We could go for a swim afterward."

I felt my mother's eyes on me, and I knew what she was thinking: Old Chip-on-the Shoulder doesn't deserve an invitation like this.

I smiled over at Andrea.

Eat your heart out, Brenda Dunlap, I thought to myself as we settled back in the taxicab. I was really looking forward to this. I had never been to a country club before. And the thought occurred to me that probably Brenda hadn't either, nor Eva Marie or Kathy or any of those . . . snobs. There it was, that word again. But I was thinking of Brenda now, not Andrea. What was happening to me?

Splashes of pink and white flowers dotted the grounds of the Club as we pulled into the circular driveway. The Club itself was a huge white mansion with a green-and-white-striped awning fluttering over the veranda.

We got out at the main entrance, and the doorman held the door open for us.

"Good morning, Miss Fairchild. Good to see the sun again, isn't it?"

"It sure is, Bill!" Andrea said, smiling up at him.

Andrea strode purposefully through a large, well-furnished lobby and then turned left down a narrow hallway. I practically had to skip to keep up with her.

"I'm sorry if I'm rushing you, but I don't want to be late."

"That's okay," I said, gasping for breath.

As we loped along I caught glimpses of the life outside through the louvered windows along the hallway. There was a large swimming pool, surrounded by gardens, and neat rows of lounge chairs were filled with deeply tanned bodies baking themselves just a little bit more.

I settled myself in a chair under a tree and watched Andrea's tennis lesson. Her instructor was named David, and he was young — about nineteen or twenty, I think — and very good looking. He laughed a lot and didn't get mad even when Andrea missed three shots in a row. He wasn't like any teacher I had ever had in my whole life.

After the lesson, Andrea said, "Were you terribly bored?"

"Uh-uh," I said truthfully, shaking my head. And then I giggled. "Who could be bored watching your tennis instructor?"

Andrea's face turned beet-red, and I knew suddenly why she was so devoted to tennis.

"He . . . he's nice, isn't he?" she said.

"He's more than nice, Andrea, and you know it!"

Her face was really crimson now, and a worried look came over it. "Please don't say anything, Fran. At home, I mean."

I couldn't figure out what she was getting at.

"Richard doesn't think David is a very good teacher. He'd rather I went with Mr. Heller. But, well, I like David. . . ."

"Of course I won't say anything, Andrea. I promise."

She looked embarrassed, and I knew suddenly that I really liked Andrea Fairchild. I liked her a lot.

She took a long drink of water from the wall fountain and said, "I don't know about you, but I'm famished. Let's have lunch before we go for a swim, okay?"

We sat at a little round table overlooking the pool, and at Andrea's suggestion, I ordered a club sandwich. It came with little fancy toothpicks in it, and I stuck them in my pocket to take home with me. I didn't know what I'd do with them, but I knew I'd want them as a souvenir.

"You can have mine if you like," Andrea offered. "I've got a whole bunch of them at home."

"That's okay," I said, and we both laughed.

The waiter treated us just like grown-ups, and I loved it. When he brought the check, Andrea signed her name to the bottom of it and I almost died.

It was then that it hit me: a moment of truth . . . a revelation! I wanted to be very rich when I grew up. I wanted to live like that, eating sandwiches with fancy toothpicks in them, and having people open doors for me, and just signing my name instead of paying real money. I wanted to have a perfect room like Andrea's, and a carousel horse all my own.

If that was being disloyal to my parents, or Sarah, or Brenda, I didn't want to think about it.

We changed into our bathing suits in the Fairchilds' cabana and spent the rest of the afternoon by the pool. Andrea wasn't a super swimmer, I was relieved to find out. I mean, she didn't spend all her time doing swan dives off the high board. She was pretty good at cannonballs, though, and we spent a lot of time doing those. I taught her how to do a handstand, and she taught me how to do a back flip.

When we got home, my mother told me Brenda had called.

"The taxi had just gone out of the driveway," she said.

"Did you tell her where I had gone?" I asked.

"Well, as a matter of fact, I did. Naturally, she was curious. I think she wanted you to go to the beach with her and Eva Marie. Why don't you give her a ring?"

I nodded and went to the phone. "Hi. Brenda?" I said, when she picked it up on the first ring.

"Cuz? How're you doing?"

"Okay."

"More than okay! I heard you went to the Country Club with Miss Moneybags. How was it?"

There was an awkward pause while I rummaged around in my brain for something to say. Finally I just blurted out the truth. "It was fabulous, Brenda. Absolutely great!"

"I bet! You've got to tell us all about it. You want to go to the beach tomorrow?"

"Sure," I said.

"Ten o'clock bus?"

"Ten o'clock."

See you then."

"So long, Brenda."

So I was going to the beach the next day with Brenda and Eva Marie. I hoped they wouldn't ask me a lot of questions about my day with Andrea. They'd just start making fun of her, and not understand at all.

I wasn't a bit sleepy, so I took a fresh piece of paper from my night-table drawer. I wrote:

Dear Sarah,

Thank you for your letter. I meant to answer right away, but things have been so hectic. You'll never guess where I went today! Give up? The Merriweather Country Club. I went with the girl that I wrote you about — the one with the carousel horse in her room. I was right about her being R-I-C-H. But so is everybody at a country club. It was absolutely unbelievable. I'll give you all the juicy details when I get home. But I know you won't believe me. If you don't, I have some toothpicks to prove it.

I think you're wrong about Charlie Bidwell being a cat lover. You're not beginning to like him, are you? UGH.

I'm sorry it's so hot in New York City. Give my love to Fluffy, Snowball, and Midnight. Write soon,

Love,

Fran

P.S. The girl that I told you is rich, is nice, *too. Although I didn't think so at first.*

There was so much I wanted to tell Sarah. . . . Maybe I'd figure out a way before I got home. I'd have to think about it.

·11·

Aunt Jessie drove us down to the station on Friday to meet the five forty-two. I was the first one to spot Dad and Steve getting off the train, and I took off like a bird and threw myself at my father, almost knocking him down.

"Hey, pumpkin! How much have you grown?" my father asked, laughing and trying to catch his breath.

Then he hugged my mother for what seemed like *forever*, while Steve and I punched each other a couple of times, just for fun. We do that sometimes when we're getting along real good. Since we hadn't seen each other for over a month, we were getting along sensationally.

Aunt Jessie had bought some steaks, and we were going to have a cookout to celebrate the Davies family's being together again. The Dunlaps have cookouts all summer long, of course, but we don't, since we live in an apartment, so it was a real treat for us.

My father put on a silly barbecue apron and made a big deal out of getting the fire going before Uncle Phil got home. When I saw him standing alone at the grill, I went out to join him. He put his arm around me and gave me a squeeze.

"How's it been, Fran?" he asked. "Tell the truth now. Has living in that big fancy house spoiled you for our little apartment?"

He was smiling, and his voice was teasing, but the question made me uncomfortable.

"Of course not!" I said earnestly. The thought was ridiculous. But I *was* beginning to realize for the first time in my life how terrific some people's lives are. The Fairchilds had so much more than we did.

"Daddy, do you like your job?" I asked, changing the subject.

"Being a pool director, you mean? Sure. It reminds me of my younger days. But I'm glad I only have a few more weeks to go. I'm afraid my brains might melt, just sitting around in the sun all day. It'll be good to get back into a classroom."

He put on a big oven mitt and poked at the fire.

"There. Old Phil's never gotten a fire going that fast in his life."

We laughed and then stood together quietly, staring at the flames.

"Do you think your mother's been happy?" he asked me, still looking at the fire.

I looked up at him. "Oh, sure," I said. "She's been having a ball. They're nice people and — well, you know Mom when she gets near a stove."

He smiled at that, and it was a nice relaxed smile. I had known my mother was worrying about my father; now I realized my father had been worrying about my mother. It felt good being able to reassure him.

Dinner was a noisy affair, with both families crowded around the picnic table and everybody laughing and talking at the same time.

Dad told a story about this big fat lady who always insisted on sitting in a tiny pool chair. One afternoon she got stuck, and Dad told Steve to pull her out. Only, after a couple of tries, Steve came back and said, "It's no use, Dad, she's in there for good. I can't get her out."

We were all laughing so hard I thought I was going to wet my pants. Can you imagine dumb Steve saying, "She's in there for *good*"? Dad said he was just grateful Steve hadn't said that to the lady. Finally, of course, he did get her out with some help from one of the lifeguards. "She's a very important woman, and I don't think she'd appreciate spending the rest of her days wedged into a pool chair."

My mother talked about some of the exotic things she had gotten a chance to cook at the Fairchilds', and I was glad that she made the job sound interesting. Then she said to Aunt Jessie, "But two weeks from now — that'll be the real test."

I stopped chewing at that remark. What was going to happen in two weeks?

"What's going to happen two weeks from now?" I asked.

"A party, that's what. A whopper wing-ding of a party."

I took a moment to disgest this bit of information. I had never thought about the Fairchilds' giving a party. With the exception of the dinner party, all they seemed to do was work. I had never seen any of their friends. In fact, I hardly ever saw *them.* I wondered idly if Mr. Fairchild would laugh, or maybe even tell jokes at a party. The few times I'd seen him he'd looked so serious.

"You're peeling," my mother said in an accusatory voice, and I snapped back to the conversation. But she was looking at Steve. Steve is much lighter than I am, and he gets lots of freckles in the summertime. He just burns and peels, burns and peels. I think he's going to run out of skin by the time he's twenty-one.

"I kept telling him to put some cream on. But he was too busy impressing the girls," my father said with a grin. I couldn't tell if Steve was blushing or not. Usually I can tell, but he was so red it was impossible.

The night was warm and muggy, so Brenda and I decided to sleep out on the screened-in porch. We gabbed for a while, then lay listening to the night noises in the woods. It was very peaceful. I even enjoyed the sound of the crickets; they didn't seem so noisy anymore. When we were little, Brenda and I used to love to sleep out on the porch, and this reminded me of those nights when we lay very quiet, listening, neither of us feeling we had to talk all the time, the way you usually do at slumber parties.

Then I remembered something I'd been meaning to tell Brenda.

"Are you awake?" I asked.

"Yeah," came a muffled voice from the pillow next to me.

"Remember how you told me that when Andrea first moved here she turned down all those invitations? Just kept saying no to everything?"

Brenda propped her head in her hands and looked at me.

"Yeah? So?"

"Well, that wasn't her fault. It was her parents. Especially her stepfather. He doesn't let her go anywhere."

"That's not true, Fran. She goes lots of places with Debbie Spencer."

"That's just it. Don't you see? The Spencers live near the Fairchilds, and they belong to the same club. So she's allowed to pal around with her."

"They must be real snobs."

I didn't know what to say to that for a moment.

"I don't think that's it exactly, Brenda. He's just overprotective, because he and Mrs. Fairchild aren't around very much."

Brenda made a grunting sound which I couldn't interpret, and then settled back down on the pillow.

I stretched my bare legs out over my sleeping bag and went back to listening to the crickets.

At about five o'clock on Saturday we decided to go to Mario's for pizza. We invited the Dunlaps to join us, but they said no, and secretly we were glad. This would be our only chance to be together, just the four of us. Dad and Steve were leaving in the morning, and it would be almost another month before we'd see them again.

Dad borrowed Uncle Phil's car, and as we pulled out of the driveway, Mom turned to me and said, "Shall we drive by the Fairchilds' so your father and Steve can see where we've been living in luxury?"

We directed my father, and soon we were on the road approaching the Fairchilds' driveway.

"Do you think we should drive in?" I asked. "You know you can't really see much from the road."

"No, I don't think we'd better," my mother said.

Just as she said that, a thin blond figure

came out from the tall hedges bordering the driveway and started walking ahead of us.

"Why, it's Andrea," my mother said, surprised. "I wonder where she's going."

We pulled to a stop alongside her, and Andrea turned to look at the car suspiciously. When she recognized my mother, she broke into a wide smile.

"Hi!" she said. "Are you back already?"

"No, dear," my mother said. "We were, uh, taking a drive. What are you doing out here?"

"Just taking a walk," Andrea said, shrugging her shoulders. She spotted me in the back of the car and waved.

"Andrea, I'd like you to meet Fran's father," my mother said.

My father got out of the car and came around and shook hands with Andrea. I noticed how much younger he looked than Mr. Fairchild. My father was really a very nice-looking man, now that I thought about it.

"Are your parents home?" my mother asked. I thought she was being pretty nosy.

"No, something came up this afternoon, and they had to go into the city. But they won't be late," Andrea assured us hastily.

I thought I heard my mother sigh. She had gotten out of the car, too, and I didn't know whether to join them or sit still. My stomach was grumbling, and I knew I'd faint if we didn't get to Mario's soon.

"Have you had your dinner?" Mom asked her.

"Not yet. But there's food in there. Maggie left some sandwiches and stuff."

There was an awkward silence, and then my father said very gallantly, "Andrea, why don't you join us? We were just driving to Mario's for pizza."

For a second I was annoyed. This was to be a family pizza, no outsiders. Even Brenda hadn't come. Then I saw Andrea's face light up as I watched through the car window, and I couldn't be mad. She was saying, "No, thank you, I wouldn't want to intrude" in a way that made you know she was dying to get away from that big empty house.

"Do you know where to reach your parents?" my mother asked her.

Andrea nodded.

"Then why don't you go and call them and ask their permission, just so they won't worry if they should telephone. Tell them we'll bring you home safe and sound."

And that's how Andrea Fairchild ended up coming for pizza with us.

Mario isn't a very fancy place, but they

have the best pizza in the whole world. We took one of the round booths in the corner, so the five of us could fit comfortably.

Right away I found out something wonderful about Andrea. She hates anchovies and loves pepperoni, just as I do. Which put another vote on my side when we were deciding what to order.

My father told the fat-lady-in-a-tiny-chair story for Andrea, and we all laughed again. Andrea seemed very impressed with my father. She wanted to know *where* he taught, and *what* he taught, and if he *enjoyed* teaching. All I could figure was that maybe she wanted to be a teacher herself someday.

After Daddy had paid the check we left Mario's and walked slowly toward the parking lot where we had left the car. We looked in store windows along the way, Mom and Dad walking in front, Steve, Andrea, and me in back. I noticed Dad putting his arm around Mom, and I realized that I had never paid any attention to that kind of thing before. Andrea was looking at them, too. I felt good seeing them walk together like that, but it was strange. Why had I never noticed it before?

·12·

I felt bad when Dad and Steve went back to the Island and Mom and I went back to the Fairchilds'. I know Mom missed them, too, but she was so busy she didn't have time to be sad. All I heard the next two weeks was the party, the party. And I had to admit it did sound exciting.

There were going to be Japanese lanterns hung on the patio and all around the property, with little candles in them that would be lit when it got dark. The guest list was for one hundred people, and my mother was in charge of everything. The Fairchilds were hiring extra help for the night of the party, but it was my mother who planned the menu and was preparing almost all the food. And she didn't seem to mind a bit. She was constantly out of breath the week before the party, and lists and reminders were tacked up everywhere. I just took off for the beach with Brenda at every opportunity and tried to stay out of her way.

I would like to be able to report that the morning of the party dawned bright and sunny and that my mother sailed through the house like the commander of a battleship in full array: barking orders, double-checking everything, smoothing out all the little last-minute wrinkles.

Unfortunately, if I'm going to be truthful, I must say it was a cloudy, threatening morning and I awoke to the sound of my mother moaning in the bathroom.

"What's the matter?" I asked, quickly jumping up and going to the open bathroom door.

"Nothing, love. I just have a headache," she said, taking some aspirin out of the medicine cabinet.

"Is that all? My gosh, I thought you were dying."

"It's good to moan when you're nervous, Fran. It releases the tension. I read that in last month's *Good Housekeeping.*" She flashed me a weak smile. "Not that I'm nervous. Not *really.*"

She walked out on the terrace, the tumbler from the bathroom still in her hand, and glancing up at the sky, she asked no one in particular, "Do you think it's going to clear up?"

Personally, I didn't think so, but I had a feeling my mother would hurl herself off the terrace dramatically (and fall two feet into a rose bush) if I said that, so I said, "Sure, it's just the early-morning fog off the Sound."

I don't know what made me come up with something so brilliant, but my mother looked so relieved as I said it that I felt extremely pleased with myself.

"What can I do to help you today?" I asked. There are times when a kid just knows that she has to sort of, well, mother a mother. And this was one of those times.

My mother smiled. "Just give me your moral support," she said, starting to make the bed. Then she stood up suddenly, looked at the ceiling, and let out another long, low moan.

I think I would make a very good weatherman — or meteorologist, as they like to be called. I'd wear big tortoise-shell glasses and be very witty and clever. And I'd be right all the time, which is more than I can say for the ones who are on TV nowadays.

The reason I am having these thoughts is because at precisely ten thirty-two the sun came out, and I heard the gardener tell my mother that "the fog sure stayed around a long time this morning!" For a city kid, I thought I had done pretty good.

As the fog lifted, so did my mother's spirits. She still wasn't exactly sailing around, but she wasn't stumbling so much, and that was an improvement.

Mrs. Fairchild came into the kitchen about three o'clock in the afternoon, and she was obviously very impressed with all the food my mother had prepared.

"Would you like to sample some of the pâté? Or the quiche?" my mother asked, fluttering over the food like a bird with a broken wing.

Mrs. Fairchild threw her hands up in mock horror. "Oh, no, you're the expert. I'm sure they're divine. You know me. I just look; I don't eat."

Andrea came into the kitchen then and let out a sigh of exasperation. "Maggie, aren't you going to eat at your own party?"

"I know what you want, pet," Mrs. Fairchild said, tweaking Andrea's nose in a way that I think annoyed Andrea. "You want your mother to be a fat old lady."

"You could never be fat, Maggie," Andrea said.

"How do we know? If I ate I might."

Andrea's mother flitted about checking everything over and letting out cries of "Lovely!" and "Magnificent!" Then she and my mother went out onto the patio to check the buffet tables.

Andrea and I were silent for a moment. Then abruptly, as if she had been debating whether to say anything or not, she said, "Are you going to help serve?"

My mouth fell open and I must have looked like a complete moron, but I just sat there for what seemed like an hour staring at her. A lot of different emotions were churning around inside me, and I wasn't sure which one was going to get the upper hand. How could I have been so dumb as to think Andrea Fairchild was anything but what Brenda said she was: a spoiled, stuck-up . . . I wanted to hiss something venomous at her about me not being a servant, and about my mother not being one either, not really, but I didn't trust myself to speak.

I shook my head quickly and ran out of the kitchen and into my room.

I didn't cry when I got to my room, but I felt like it. I really had begun to like Andrea, and not just because I was lonely. I had thought we were friends.

There was a timid knock at the door, and when I opened it and saw Andrea standing there I couldn't have been more surprised. I thought for a moment, She's come to apologize for treating me like a maid! And then I thought, I won't accept her apology. I can be just as cool and aloof as she is. But while I was thinking these thoughts she sauntered past me and flopped on my bed as if she owned the place — which, of course, she did.

"Are you sure you don't want to serve?" she asked, acting as though I were being a real spoilsport.

I swallowed hard and controlled myself admirably. "No, Andrea, I do not want to serve. And I don't know what makes you think I have to!"

She got up then, looking really annoyed. "You don't have to. Of course you don't *have* to. But what are you going to do with one hundred people crawling all over the place? Maggie and Richard won't let me be at their parties unless I get into something fancy and pass hors d'oeuvres like a little darling. Then I get to stay at the party and eat all the stuff and listen to them talk. They're crazy! Honest, Fran, a lot of the people who come are really crazy. I thought if you have a long dress, we could both help and it would be fun. I stayed up till twelve thirty last time."

"Oh . . . I said. "You mean, together, we . . . oh . . ." I felt ashamed of what I had been thinking.

"Will you? Please? It'll be fun, I promise."

"Well, sure," I said. "But I don't have anything fancy to wear."

"Come up to my room and we'll find something. We must be the same size."

I had only been in Andrea's room a few times since that first day when I saw the carousel horse. It was still there, of course, standing sentry by the window. And once again I stared at it, and a wave of envy swept over me.

Andrea opened her closet and pulled out a yellow two-piece outfit. "Here's something that would look really super on you," she said.

On closer scrutiny, I realized it was hip-hugger pants with a tiny halter top. I shook my head violently. "I couldn't wear that," I said.

"Why not?" she asked innocently.

I started to giggle. "My belly button is funny looking," I said truthfully.

Andrea let out a roar. "You, too? That's why I never wear it. Or bikinis, either."

I was laughing out loud now. "I guess we'll never be sex symbols."

"Maggie says I'm silly. But she likes to wear things like that. My mother has five bikinis."

"Well, your mother has a very good figure," I said.

"Mm . . ." Andrea said, and then, as if she wanted to change the subject, she went back to the closet and pulled out a long red-and-white-checked dress with a big white apron and puffy sleeves. "This is too short on me now, so it should be just right on you," she said. I would rather have served in my cutoffs and a T-shirt, but the dress had a colonial look, and if I had to wear something fancy, it wasn't too bad.

"I'll meet you downstairs at five o'clock," Andrea said, and I took the dress back to my room.

When I went into the kitchen at five o'clock,

Andrea was there already, sampling one of the canapés. She looked really nice in a long white organdy dress.

Then Mr. Fairchild came in, and I almost fainted. He didn't look anything like the Mr. Fairchild I had seen off and on over the summer — the one in the dark suit with the attaché case in his hand.

He had sandals on his feet, and was wearing orange pants and a shirt with orange and yellow flowers on it. Around his neck (where the shirt was unbuttoned to show a lot of fuzzy white hair) he had hung a medallion. The thought occurred to me that Mrs. Fairchild would have a hard time competing for the title of "most beautiful person at the party."

Just as I was thinking that, in came Andrea's mother. And was I wrong! She was wearing a yellow floating kind of thing, and — are you ready? — had two giant yellow flowers behind her ears. I couldn't tell right away whether her outfit was one piece or two pieces, but it was gorgeous. And as she brushed by me I could smell the flowers in her hair, and I realized they were *real*. That fascinated me. How did they stay fresh? I'd have to remember to ask Andrea about that. I suddenly felt good, knowing that I could ask

Andrea things and that we could talk, nice and regular.

I felt a twinge for a moment, remembering that my mother would be wearing the little blue number again. But then I realized suddenly, and very, very clearly, that it really wasn't that important. In any uniform, I would still choose my mother over the apparition that had just floated past.

Now the guests started arriving. I'd never seen so many people in one house at one time. There was a bar set up inside and a bar set up outside. Pretty soon everybody was edging past everybody else, and they were all laughing their heads off. The men looked very fancy, every bit as fancy as the women. And Andrea hadn't been exaggerating when she said some of them were really crazy. There was a woman there who had rings on every single finger, even her thumbs, and several people who wore sunglasses even though it was getting dark and all the Japanese lanterns were lit. There was a very bony girl who looked awfully familiar, and Andrea told me she was a famous model who did TV commercials.

I had never realized before how dull all my parents' friends were.

I don't think Andrea and I were really

needed, because another woman was there besides my mother, and most of the food was on a long table on the terrace. But Andrea and I passed the hors d'oeuvres just to get our hands on them. I've never eaten so much.

Then we went and ruined the whole thing. There was this bowl of guacamole — that's a real messy kind of dip that I don't especially like. It's a sickly green color because it's made with avocados. Andrea was crazy about it and insisted on passing it around. The trouble was, the bowl was heavy, and you needed two hands to carry it. So she carried the bowl and I carried another bowl with crackers in it.

Anyway, there was this very weird guy, who, Andrea said, was a well-known dancer. He must have been talking about dancing a lot, because he was always jumping around while he talked. He was one of the men who had their shirts all unbuttoned and wore lots of beads. Anyway, he must have been making a point about something, because just as Andrea and I came up behind him he spun around real fast, waving his hand wildly in the air. Andrea was just about to offer the dip, and . . . well, I know this sounds disgusting, but his hand landed right in the guacamole. He looked absolutely horrified. And

Andrea and I got absolutely hysterical. I started laughing something fierce, and the bowl of crackers I was holding started to shake and some of the crackers fell out.

Luckily my mother saw what had happened, and she hurried over with a napkin. The dancer took the napkin and staggered out to wash his green hand, holding it dramatically in front of him, as if he were afraid it was going to drop off.

My mother gave us a withering look, which I suppose she felt she had to, but I think she knew it wasn't our fault. However, it did draw attention to us, and that wasn't good. In a few minutes Andrea's mother suggested that it was getting late, and that we ought to get to bed.

We weren't a bit sleepy, so we went to Andrea's room and watched from the window. I tried hard to take in all the colors and the people and the silly things that were happening so I could tell Sarah all about it when I got back home. It would be tricky explaining to her how I happened to be at the party till past midnight. But nobody else seemed to care that my mother was a cook, not Dad, or Andrea, or Brenda, so it was beginning not to matter to me either.

I felt a poke in my side and looked to where Andrea was pointing.

"Look at *those*," she said, pointing to a plate of cream puffs my mother had just added to the buffet. "Don't they look divine?"

"Oh, and they *are*, Andrea! She makes them for our parties at home!" Suddenly I was absolutely starved.

"I bet there's more in the kitchen," Andrea said, in a tone of voice that told me she was throwing caution to the wind.

"Do we dare?" I said nervously.

Andrea fixed me with a determined stare. "Fran, we've eaten an awful lot of spicy food tonight, and I don't know about you, but my stomach is beginning to feel queasy."

I stared at her openmouthed. "Gee, you *look* all right."

She let out a long sigh. "This is our cover story, silly. Would your mother want us to be up here throwing up all over the place? Of course not. What I need is a nice glass of milk. Don't you? I mean, how can they object to us going into the kitchen for a nice wholesome glass of milk?"

We got up and started toward the door. "But, Andrea," I thought suddenly, "I don't want just a glass of milk."

She turned and stared at me as though I were the most hopeless person she had ever had to sneak into a kitchen with.

"Oh, of course," I said. "That's our *cover* story."

We went downstairs quietly and listened. Sounds of laughter and loud conversation drifted in from the garden, but the kitchen was deathly still. We hurried in and searched about frantically for the cream puffs.

"You pour two glasses of milk, while I look," Andrea said.

Feeling like a burglar, I did as I was told, and was just about to put the milk back when the door to the garden opened.

"Right in here, Igor. I'm so *sorry,*" Mrs. Fairchild was saying.

"It's my fault, Mrs. Fairchild. I shouldn't have put the bowl where I did," my mother added.

It was the dancer again, and this time his fingers were dripping with some kind of white sauce as they led him to the sink.

Standing there, trapped as we were, with me still holding the bottle of milk, Andrea and I were helpless to do anything but stare at the scene in front of us.

Then, as if someone had pressed a button,

we started to giggle. The giggles grew into laughter, and the laughter into loud snorts until tears were coming out of our eyes.

Mrs. Fairchild noticed us then, of course, and she looked furious.

"You two are supposed to be in your beds!" she said.

My mother had given the dancer a towel to dry his hands on, and as he started back out to the party, Mrs. Fairchild quickly followed him, mumbling condolences.

Mom just looked at us for a moment.

"We . . . we just came down to get a glass of milk, Mrs. Davies," Andrea said.

I poked her in the ribs. "Tell her about our stomachs," I said.

"Oh . . . and yeah, our stomachs were queasy," she added.

"I see. Well, put the milk back in the refrigerator before you go upstairs," my mother said, turning toward the door. And then, without turning or breaking her stride, she added, "They're on the third shelf, right behind the butter."

They were. And they were delicious.

·13·

Dear Sarah,

Thank you for your letter, which I got yesterday.

A new *Charlie Bidwell?? I hope you're right, but this I've got to see. Anyway, I don't mind so much if you gave him Midnight. Everyone knows black cats are bad luck.*

It doesn't seem possible that the summer is almost over, but here it is the middle of August already. We'll be back in school before we know it! Ugh . . .

My cousin Brenda is planning a big sleepover. Maybe ten or twelve kids, and no one's allowed to go to sleep the whole night. I'm really looking forward to it. Wish me luck!

I really miss you and can't wait to get back to good old New York City. Has it changed much?

See you soon!

Love,
Fran

Things were pretty sticky around the house for a few days after the party. My mother gave me a lecture about embarrassing people and stuff like that. I don't know what Andrea's parents said to her. She didn't say anything, but since they were awfully busy all the time, maybe she didn't get into any trouble at all.

One afternoon my mother said casually, "Fran, did I tell you where the Fairchilds are going next week?"

I shook my head.

"Rome."

"Rome, *Italy?* Wow."

"Isn't that exciting?"

"Is Andrea going?"

"*No.*" My mother frowned, as if that were a ridiculous idea. "It's business, dear."

"Oh," I said. They were always going places without her. "When are they coming back?"

"The end of the month. They'll be back about the same time as Bertha. That's when we'll leave."

The day the Fairchilds left for Rome was a gloomy, chilly day. The limousine picked them up at noon, and for the next couple of hours Andrea seemed to have vanished.

"Have you seen Andrea?" I asked my mother.

"No, I haven't. Have you looked in her room?"

The door to Andrea's room was closed. I hesitated for a moment, and then I tapped softly.

"Come in," Andrea answered immediately.

I poked my head in the door. "Are you sleeping?" I asked.

"No, of course not. I was just reading."

"That's why I came upstairs. Could I borrow a book? I haven't anything to read."

"Of course."

I scanned the bookshelf for a moment in silence.

"Your parents must be excited, going to Rome," I said finally, just to make conversation.

"Not really. They go a lot."

"Maybe sometime you'll get to go, too."

"Oh, I really don't think I'd enjoy it. Business trips are a bore. Everyone knows that."

It was as if there were two Andreas: one was cold and aloof, the other friendly and warm. Now that I had gotten to know what I liked to think was the real Andrea, this one didn't bother me so much. I realized now that this was just an act. I think she wanted to cover up how she really felt, instead of crying, or acting like a brat (which is what I would do).

I picked out *Anne's House of Dreams* and turned toward the door.

"When is Brenda's sleepover going to be?" she asked suddenly.

I had mentioned the sleepover casually to Andrea one afternoon, but I hadn't gone into very much detail, since we both knew she wasn't going to be invited.

"Tomorrow night," I said.

"I bet you're looking forward to it."

"Mm-m."

"Who's going to be there?"

"Oh, you know, the usual gang," I said evasively.

"Eva Marie Schwartzkopf?"

"Sure. She's Brenda's best friend."

Andrea closed her book and lay back with her head propped on her elbow.

"I think that's one girl I would really enjoy at a sleepover."

"How come?" I asked, puzzled.

"Because she can't talk when she's asleep, can she?" I laughed and she continued. "Though come to think of it, she probably talks in her sleep, in that lovely voice of hers." And Andrea held her nose so that her voice came out amazingly like Eva Marie's.

"Do you really think she talks in her sleep?" I said, both fascinated and horrified at the thought.

"Probably. Or maybe she just snores."

Well, that did it, because Brenda had told me once how Eva Marie *did* snore one night at a slumber party and kept everybody awake. I started to giggle, and then Andrea started to giggle, and neither of us could stop. And we didn't really know what we were laughing about.

Finally I started out the door, and Andrea followed me out to the stairway with a suddenly serious look on her face, as if she were thinking hard about something. She leaned over the banister as I started down the stairs.

"Fran?"

I stopped and looked back at her.

"Why don't *we* have a sleepover?"

"Really?"

"Why not? This has been such a *boring* day! We could get tons of food and stay up as late as we like. Let's do it tonight, *please?*"

I nodded my head. "Sure, I said. A sleepover in that perfect room with the carousel horse! I bounded down the stairs to tell my mother and see what was in the refrigerator for a midnight snack.

Brenda called at exactly four thirty-five.

"Tonight's the night!" she yelled into the phone.

"What?"

"I had to switch it. My dad's going to be out of town tonight, instead of tomorrow night, so my mother made me change it."

"But . . . I can't come *tonight*."

"Fran Davies, what do you mean, you can't? What do you have, a date or something?"

I hesitated a moment.

"I'm having a sleepover with Andrea," I said.

"What? You're kidding."

"No, honest. She just asked me."

"Well, make it another night. Make it tomorrow."

I was silent for a moment. I could do that. I could go right upstairs and explain everything and just postpone it until tomorrow. But at the same time I knew I just couldn't.

"Brenda, I can't. That wouldn't be fair. I already promised, when I thought your sleepover was going to be tomorrow." I almost said, Andrea's *lonely*, Brenda, but I stopped myself. I didn't think Andrea would want me to say that, and besides, that really didn't have anything to do with my decision.

"Oh, Fran, that's lousy. I think you just prefer her house, if you want to know what I think."

"That's not true, and you know it."

"Well, I can't stay on this phone all night begging you. I've got a lot of phone calls to make. Are you sure you can't come?"

"Honest, Brenda, I'd love to. You know that. I'm real sorry."

"So long." And I heard a click before I could say "so long" back.

Boy, did I feel funny. On the one hand I felt very noble and virtuous, but on the other hand, I felt terrible about feeling noble and virtuous. It wasn't as if I were making a sacrifice by giving up Brenda's party. No, I really preferred Andrea's company. But that made me feel guilty, because Brenda was my cousin. Then I told myself it had nothing to do with Brenda, exactly. It was all those other girls that I hardly knew. No, I was definitely more comfortable with Andrea.

We took two Cokes, a bag of potato chips, and a batch of cookies up to Andrea's room about nine o'clock. We got into our pajamas, and I climbed into the canopied bed with a Coke in one hand and a handful of potato chips in the other. Immediately I knew I'd made a mistake. Andrea's sheets were trimmed with genuine, thick lace, with thin strips of yellow velvet ribbon running through it. Did Queen Elizabeth eat potato chips in bed? I hardly thought so. I got out and sat on the floor in front of the television set. (Of course she had her own television.)

As always, I find it hard to describe that girl's room. It was just perfect. There was one whole wall of closets, right? And everything in the closet was gorgeous, with a special place for everything: shoes in shoe boxes, belts on special hooks, and a whole row of shelves with fluffy sweaters neatly folded inside plastic bags. The inside of the closet was even wallpapered and carpeted like the rest of the room!

"How can you keep everything so neat?" I finally asked. I still felt a little uncomfortable with someone who obviously hung up her clothes as a matter of routine, and not just because it was the end of the week.

"If you had Maggie and Richard breathing down your neck, you would too!" she said. "I tried the sloppy routine, and on top of everything else, it just made everything too . . . yuk."

She checked herself then, as if she had said too much. And frankly, I wasn't sure I knew what she was talking about anyway.

About eleven o'clock we started watching a horror movie, and we both got scared out of our wits. It was about a man who had killed his wife and stuffed the body in a trunk in the attic. I had goose bumps all over me. Attics have always sounded very scary to me. And I made the mistake of saying so to Andrea.

"Ours isn't," she said, shaking her head, as we turned off the TV.

"You have an attic?" I said, and immediately realized it was a dumb thing to say. I always imagine attics to be in creaky, spooky old houses. I guess most houses have them, but I couldn't picture one in a big, elegant house like this.

"I *love* my attic," Andrea said softly. "It's my favorite place in the house."

I thought maybe she was just teasing me, but then I realized she was serious.

"That's where all my favorite things are," she went on. "Not beautiful things, like down here, but favorite. Would you like to come and see?"

Well, needless to say, I did not want to come and see any attic. I half suspected that was the invitation the man in the movie had given his wife, just before he grabbed his hatchet.

"I don't think your folks would want us to go prowling around in the attic in the middle of the night," I said, shaking my head soberly. My spine was turning to jelly just at the thought.

"Oh, Fran, don't be such a scaredy-cat. My folks aren't home, and your mother wouldn't hear us. Besides, you'll like it, I promise you."

Even as she was saying that, she had jumped up and taken a flashlight out of the drawer in her night table. She opened the door and turned the flashlight on, lighting up the hallway.

"Come on," she said, as if the decision had been made and there was just no way out of it.

I got up reluctantly, *very* reluctantly, and followed Andrea. She started toward the end of the hall where the den was. You couldn't hear a sound as our bare feet sank into the thick hall carpeting. It had been quiet just like this in the movie, when that horrible man had grabbed the hatchet and started hunting for his wife. I remembered the scene . . .

blood dripping through from the attic, staining the ceiling . . . and I looked up convulsively. But it was so dark I couldn't even tell if there *was* a ceiling. Oh, to be walking nice and safe down some dark street in New York City!

"Could you walk a little closer to me with that flashlight?" I called after Andrea, who seemed to have gotten miles ahead of me.

"Just a second, I'll switch on a light," she said.

But instead I heard the creak of a door being opened. Visions of creaking doors and cobwebs and bony hands, phantoms from all the scary movies I had ever watched, leaped about in the hallway. Then suddenly it was light, and I saw that Andrea had opened a door and was starting up a steep, narrow staircase. I wasn't about to be left in the dark hallway by myself, so I scrambled up after her.

I was so surprised when I reached the top of the stairs that I heard a long "Oh . . ." from somewhere, and realized it was me saying it, standing there with my mouth open.

The room was painted white, and was very bare as rooms go, with a ceiling that peaked in the middle. I could stand up straight in it, but most grown-ups wouldn't have been able to. The air wasn't very fresh, but just as I was thinking that, Andrea went over and switched on a fan in the wall, and it immediately began to circulate the air and make it cooler.

There were boxes of things everywhere, and some furniture, all of it white — the kind of furniture you use in a little girl's room, with pink roses painted on the knobs of the dresser drawers and on the head of the bed. There was a plain white sheet covering the mattress on the bed, and sitting up on it were three rag dolls, not very fancy or beautiful — the kind that look as if they've been loved very roughly.

"This used to be my stuff," Andrea said, opening one of the drawers and taking out some things and examining them: a pincushion in the shape of a poodle, a jar of seashells, a doll's blanket, a few books.

I walked over and picked up one of the dolls.

"That's Jessica," Andrea said shyly. "She was my favorite doll."

"If you still like this stuff, why don't you keep it in your room?" I asked, thinking at the same time how strange the three dolls would look on the elegant canopied bed.

"No . . . I'm too old for these things," she

said, "and besides, I don't like to mix *then* and *now*. It makes Maggie and Richard happy to see everything in my room new and perfect."

I sat down on the bed and motioned to the cartons.

"What's in those?"

Andrea shrugged. "That's some of the stuff I don't have room for: games Richard keeps getting me, things like that. That's *now* stuff," she said, tossing it off as if it didn't matter.

"Andrea," I said, "I don't really understand. When you say *then* and *now*, what do you mean?"

She laughed self-consciously and took a deep breath. "See, we used to live in Ohio — when I was little. My real father was a teacher in Akron."

This bit of information really floored me, but I didn't say anything. I didn't want to interrupt.

She went on. "When my folks were divorced — that was when I was seven — I went with my mother to New York. She was being transferred there with the company. And for a while I flew back and forth to visit my father. That was part of the agreement. But then they decided it was too much of a hassle for me. Besides, Maggie was marrying Richard and my father was getting married again. . . ." Her voice trailed off for a moment. Then she continued. "He lives in California now, and he has a little boy named Billy. I spent Christmas with them last year."

I didn't say anything. I just couldn't. And then when I did speak, do you know what I said?

"You have such a *beautiful* home," I mumbled, hoping that Andrea couldn't read my mind, because while I was saying it, I was thinking about my apartment and how lucky I was, and about how bad I felt for Andrea.

"I know," she said, in that clipped tone of voice. She stood on the stairway, waiting for me to descend before she flipped off the light.

We talked for a while, just about silly things, and then we went to bed. But I didn't go to sleep right away. I lay under the lacy sheets staring at the shadowy figure of the carousel horse. It was still beautiful, I suppose, but somehow it didn't seem gentle anymore.

·14·

"*Mein An-dre-a!*" boomed the voice from the kitchen doorway.

Yes, Bertha had returned, and I must admit that she was everything that Andrea had said she was: a mountain in an apron. No wonder the Fairchilds had such a large kitchen!

Andrea allowed herself to be clutched to Bertha's enormous bosom, and then stood for inspection while Bertha remarked how she had grown. Changed. Gotten *thinner*.

I saw my mother wince at the last remark, but Andrea and I just giggled.

It had been a hectic morning. In one hour Aunt Jessie would arrive to take us to the station. But I was all packed, so while Bertha and my mother had coffee, Andrea and I went up to her room.

The Fairchilds had been delayed a few days, and I knew that it bothered Andrea, but I also knew better than to say anything about it. We'd never talked about the things in the attic and what they meant. I'd wanted to, and I hoped someday we would, but not now.

Andrea shut the door behind us and sat down on the bed with a look on her face that said she was dying to tell me something.

"Fran?" she said.

"Hm?" I was browsing around the room for the last time, admiring the little glass figures on the bookshelf.

"You have a birthday in September, right?"

"Yes . . . but how did you know?"

"Don't you remember we were talking about birthstones one day, and I said mine was emerald because I've got a May birthday, and you said yours was sapphire because you were born in September?"

"That's right."

"Well, I've been trying to think of something I could send you that I'd be sure you'd like. And I think I've got it."

She paused while my mind raced around, trying to imagine what it could be.

"What do I have that I know you'd really, truly like to have?"

I thought for a moment. And then I caught the look on Andrea's face. She was glancing first at me and then at . . . the carousel horse.

"Andrea . . ."

"Would your parents let you keep it in your apartment?"

"Oh, Andrea, I couldn't!"

"But you're crazy about Amber. I know you are! I'd really like you to have her."

I walked slowly over to the corner and looked at the smooth golden neck and the snowy mane. Then I looked at the eyes. Had they changed? Could Amber have changed over the summer? I thought of the first day I had seen her and of how I had envied a girl who could possess such a fabulous thing. And I thought of the night I had slept here, and how firece the horse had looked in the moonlight.

I stroked the painted head and turned to Andrea. "It's really super of you to consider giving Amber to me. But I couldn't take her. I just couldn't."

The carousel horse was no longer a symbol of everything fantastic and unattainable. It stood there now reminding me of everything that Andrea had lost. I had thought my family was being broken apart, just because we were separated for a little while. How wrong I had been! We were a whole, Mom, Dad, Steve, and me. And I felt somehow that we always would be.

"Do you know what I'd really like for my birthday?" I asked Andrea. The idea had been in the back of my mind for days, and suddenly it seemed the right moment to bring it out.

"What?"

"Would you come and spend a weekend in the city with me? I'd like you to see where I live, and meet my friends."

"Gee, I'd love to, Fran. But I don't know. You know how Richard is about letting me go anywhere."

"But he *knows* my mother. I'll have my father call him, too. We'd have a ball!"

"Oh, Fran, I'd love that."

"We'll work it out, Andrea. We just have to."

We said good-bye on the front driveway, with Bertha looming in the doorway, counting the minutes until she would once again be in charge of little Andre-a's stomach.

My mother hugged Andrea, and we promised to write to each other right away. I would have liked her to ride to the station with us, but since Aunt Jessie was driving, my mother said it wouldn't be fair to ask her to take Andrea all the way home again.

Brenda and I scrunched down in the back seat with the luggage, and as I waved to Andrea through the window, I thought back to the day we arrived in Merriweather and to that lonely drive from the station. The silence between Andrea and me in the back seat of that little sports car had seemed so ominous. Who would have believed that I would come to like the aloof, polished girl so much, and that we'd end the summer as real friends?

I smiled contentedly over at my counsin. "Brenda," I said, "remember I told you about Andrea, and how it was her stepfather's fault that she had to say no to so many things?"

"Yeah."

"Well, have you thought about it? Have you told the other kids?"

"No . . . I sort of forgot about it."

"Well, would you? Andrea's real nice, Brenda, and I know if you got to know her, you'd like her."

"I'm not so sure about that."

"You know me, Brenda, right? I'm your

own cousin. And I say if you got to know her, you'd like her. *I* do. Honest."

"What do you want me to do?"

"Just give her a chance. Maybe she'll never be allowed to come to sleepovers and things, but be nice to her in school."

"Okay, cuz. As a favor to you, I'll try. And I'll tell the kids about her stepfather, too."

"Thanks, Brenda. You'll be glad you did. I know you will."

We pulled into the station, and Aunt Jessie and Brenda waited with us until the train chugged to a halt in front of us. Everybody hugged everybody else, the porter helped us on with our bags, and suddenly it was all over.

On the way home I rode backwards, pressing my forehead against the window so I could watch as Merriweather retreated behind us.

My mother sat opposite me. Our eyes met, and we smiled at each other.

"The summer really went fast, didn't it?"

"Yeah, it did," I said.

"And it wasn't too bad, after all, was it?"

"No, Mom," I answered truthfully, "it wasn't bad at all."

"Did I tell you about the phone call I got from Mrs. Karsell?" she asked casually.

I was beginning to realize that when my mother asked questions like that, she knew very well that she hadn't told me, and that she had deliberately waited for this particular moment to bring up the subject.

I shook my head. "Who's Mrs. Karsell?"

"She's a friend of the Fairchilds. She was at the party, but she lives in New York, in a brownstone on East Seventy-Eighth Street."

I waited. Why would she be calling my mother?

"She offered me a job," my mother said finally.

My heart sank. Here we go again, I thought. We'll become gypsies, living out of suitcases, constantly traveling as my mother cooks her way up the ladder of success.

But I'd grown up a lot, and I just smiled and said, "Oh?" That was really all I trusted myself to say.

"She thought the food I fixed for the party was terrific. She's giving a party next month, and she wants me to cater it."

"Cater it?"

"Yes. As a matter of fact, she mentioned a friend of hers who might need my services, too. It's occurred to me that this might be the beginning of a nice little business."

I smiled brightly. "You mean you'd be a regular businesswoman!"

"I guess so. But I'd still be cooking, Fran. Let's face it, that's my 'thing,' as they say. Will it be so different from cooking exclusively for the Fairchilds? Am I any less a person because I was someone's cook for the summer?"

"Of course not." The thought was ridiculous. We smiled across at each other, and I wondered if she knew how proud I was of her. I was beginning to think I had a very liberated mother.

I couldn't wait to get home and tell Sarah.